GOLDI'S TRAVELS

A spiritual odyssey of personal discovery, *Goldi's Travels* tells of a simple Ainu fisherman who leaves his island home driven by a desire to see and experience far more than his friends, relatives and ancestors. However, even he does not expect that his travels will take him to mainland Japan, America and even England. He often finds the customs and attitudes of other races perplexing and sometimes intimidating, but comes across kindness and generosity in equal measure.

A social commentary and a spiritual journey rolled into one, this book is guaranteed to raise the spirits and rekindle a sense of hope and optimism in all its readers.

GOLDI'S TRAVELS

John Young

Book Guild Publishing
Sussex, England

First published in Great Britain in 2009 by
The Book Guild Ltd
Pavilion View
19 New Road
Brighton, BN1 1UF

Typesetting in Garamond by
SetSystems Ltd, Saffron Walden, Essex

Printed in Great Britain by
CPI Antony Rowe

A catalogue record for this book is
available from the British Library

ISBN 978 1 84624 363 9

Chapter One

There was now enough heat in the sun to make travelling pleasant without it being too hot. Goldi was wearing his summer suit, but had also brought the clothes made of thicker skins. The nights were still cold out at sea. The boat was handling easy now, so he was just letting the wind take it where it would.

Now that his grandmother was dead he felt free to go where he liked for as long as he liked. The people back in the village could not easily criticise his behaviour. He had carried out all the duties that were expected of a devoted son and had held an impressively large mourning party for the many friends and the few relatives. The carved bear cups had been passed and filled many times. After the appropriate offerings to the gods they had soon been emptied again.

Goldi was a big man for one of his race, being nearly six feet tall and strongly built. Now aged thirty-three he was in good health with all his teeth and only a small patch of baldness on the crown of his head. He also tended to be a bit thick round the waist. That was most likely due to his liking for rice beer and saké. Then again he enjoyed thinking more than hard work. It was his enquiring mind and extra height that marked him out from his fellows. That had never bothered him

1

however, as he had grown up the only child of devoted parents, or to be exact, grandparents.

He could feel the sun playing on the top of his head now, so he got out from one of his bundles a small cap which, like the suit, he had made himself from fine leather. Unlike the suit this had no decorations, so it merged with his brown hair. He also now thought it time to eat and took some food from another bundle. It was plain fare, tofu – that is, white bean curd he had grilled before leaving – and dried fish. This was quite adequate on a warm day. He washed this down with some beer. He knew he had enough supplies for five or six days. He could always supplement this with freshly caught fish. He was adept with spear and line and could also get oysters. There were shellfish including crabs from the right spots. Omu and its familiar fishing grounds were now behind him. Only once did he see some green hills on his right where a headland protruded. He did not know where he would sleep that night, but all the things he valued were now with him in the boat.

The only thing Goldi had left behind was the thatched hut that had for so long been his home. This day provided such easy sailing that after a while he thought he might as well have a drink of something stronger. Often it needed all his skill and strength to control the small craft. Today he could relax, so he had his first long drink from the saké bottle, then another.

His earliest memories had been of helping his grandparents with the few crops they grew near the hut. He also remembered chasing hens and puppies when they came anywhere near him. Sometimes he had been taken out in one of the fishing boats which were made from hollowed-out logs. When he got older, as a rare treat, he went with a hunting party armed with bows and arrows in search of deer and other game. During the long, cold winters only the hardiest could do much out of doors. Inside, with the all-pervading smell of the open fire, Goldi learnt from his grandparents. His grandfather mainly taught him carving, but he also tried to learn cooking, weaving and decorating items from his grandmother. Sometimes when he was small he said he would like a coloured moustache like hers. She had smiled and said when he was a man he could grow a fine beard like granddad.

He never felt lonely as he grew up, but wanted to learn as much as he possibly could. At the age of twelve he became betrothed to Fugi. She was one of the girls he had known since childhood. This had all been arranged between his grandparents and the girl's parents. It was then understood they would marry before the age of twenty. Although the young people met frequently at each other's houses this betrothal meant little to Goldi until he was fifteen and she was just past thirteen.

'I want a necklace like my big sister,' Fugi said one day. He just remembered seeing a string of seashells around that girl's neck a week or so earlier. Then Fugi said, 'If we go along the beach tomorrow we could collect the sizes I want, then you could make me one.'

Goldi was in truth more interested in the contents of shells than their exteriors, but he agreed, to keep her happy. The next day they took a little food with them and started working their way along the beaches. He could have collected enough shells for a necklace without losing sight of the village, but Fugi was very particular. She wanted them ranging from very small to medium-large and in particular colours. As usual he did not bother to argue. He often went along with

3

other people's ways, even if he did not really agree with them. When he was alone again he could experiment and maybe come up with something better.

Fugi finally had all the shells she wanted and they tied them into a piece of skin for safety. The sun was now quite hot, so they climbed the wooded slope to find somewhere shady to eat their food. That was soon eaten as they had healthy appetites and were at ease with each other. Fugi then started talking about when they got married. Could he build her a nice hut like the one her sister had? He said yes, if some of the other men were willing to help. Would he go hunting for their food? Goldi said he would sometimes, but he preferred to fish. This made sense as they were near the sea and he loved boats. Would he get her a hibachi like the one her aunt had? This aunt was married to a Japanese man. Fugi said then she would be able to cook quite easily all year round whatever the weather. Goldi was more cautious over this one. He knew those things cost a fair amount of money, as did the charcoal they used up all the time.

Finally he said, 'Yes, if we can afford it.'

As she carried on talking Goldi let it flow over him. He was lying back relaxed when he realised she had stopped talking and was now nibbling at his cheek. He did not mind that, as it was pleasant just being petted. However she now started fondling him and he was suddenly very wide awake. When they left their shady spot about an hour later he was fully aware what betrothal and marriage might entail. This had been a new experience for him, but life would not be so simple in the future.

There were to be two other events which were to affect him before they got married; one of these was his friendship with Okawa. By the age of sixteen Goldi

4

was already taller than most of his race and strong with it. Fishing was normally done two to a boat, either two men or husband and wife. On this occasion Goldi had decided to go out alone, confident in himself and the craft. He managed well in the strong breeze going out, but on the return it had developed into a gale and he was driven onto a strange stretch of beach. There were sampans beached there. Men were making their matting sails secure from the probing fingers of the wind. One or two glanced at him with his dugout, but they were too busy working to pay more attention. Just before he hit the beach a figure came out from behind some boats that were well up out of the way. Goldi had already jumped out into the foaming water and was trying to stop his craft getting damaged. The stranger took this in, then came hurrying down. With this help Goldi was able use a big wave to get his boat up and well out of trouble. After recovering a bit he tried to thank his rescuer, but had difficulty, knowing few words of Japanese. His meaning was clear however and when he offered five freshly caught fish they were accepted with a smile. Soon they exchanged names and Okawa indicated Goldi should follow him. As the waves still pounded the beach there was no reason to demur. Then he soon found himself sitting shoeless on the floor of a Japanese house. After some animated discussion between his new friend and his mother, peace descended. Soon they were drinking green tea and eating snacks containing crisp seaweed. Goldi had noticed Okawa walked with a limp and that one of his legs was thinner than the other. This made him admire the courage of the slim young man who had helped him all the more.

These two young men could not converse much, but Goldi found after a while that he knew more

Japanese words than he had thought. About an hour later a man came in who was obviously the father. Goldi then stood in respect while the son rattled on for some time in their own language. The father's frown faded and at last he nodded in understanding at the unusual incident that had thrown an Ainu his son's way. Shortly after all this Goldi bowed awkwardly to the parents and then left the room with Okawa. The wind had died down quite a lot now. Goldi was shown the boats that Okawa spent his time repairing. A bit later he said his thanks once more and then was able to get into his boat for home.

He reached there with no more problems except from the old couple. They had known he was out in the terrible weather and of course had thought the worst had happened. On top of that Fugi seemed very annoyed as well. To calm their fears he agreed he would not go out on any more long fishing trips on his own. That did not stop him visiting Okawa however, as that was only a short way up the coast. Goldi found that his new friend was not just a boat repairer, but was skilled at making new craft. He needed some help with the heavier work and Goldi was very pleased to assist and learn. As Okawa spoke none of the Ainu tongue he was also teaching Goldi Japanese the best way – by using it for everyday tasks. After quite some time and experiment these two were able to make a very neat little boat. We would call it a labour-saving craft. One very useful item was a sail that could still work when the wind was in the wrong quarter. Other local craft did not have that and paddling was needed. This one should be useable in all but dead calm. When it was finally completed the boat was left in Okawa's keeping, but he seldom ventured far on his own. Together they did quite long trips and once they took Fugi with them so that she could appreciate what all those extra hours of work had created. She seemed to get used to the idea of their companionship and knew that Goldi was less likely to get into trouble if he was with Okawa. After that the two friends even showed off the craft to Goldi's old folk.

In their village of old traditions this newer design helped to raise the opinion of Goldi; it was also because of the boat he met Miss Jenkins. Goldi had seen few Americans, as they lived away from any tourist centres. The odd one or two who did pass through their village generally had a special reason. Goldi remembered that when he was a small child they nearly all seemed to wear a light brown uniform.

One morning on the beach near Goldi's village he was told a new American woman had been seen wandering in very deserted parts. Locals wondered if she was a bit mad, being rather thin and untidy. Some men fishing had seen her picking up items near the high water mark and studying them through a strong glass. She would then either discard them, or put them into a travelling box she had. As the things were not likely to be edible they just smiled to themselves. A while after this Goldi saw some men talking at the end of the boats pulled up out of the sea. The woman was there and hands were pointed out to sea. When some men came away Goldi heard that she was collecting some sort of fossils. She had travelled to various countries doing this, but it was not clear why. Apparently a few bits she had found seemed to excite her enough to want to explore some of the small islands not too far away. Okawa and Goldi thought this a strange interest but she was willing to pay good money. After speaking to all the fishermen she slowly came up to them. She was obviously disappointed no one was interested. It was likely they were more worried about being laughed at by their peers than any physical concern. When she got closer to them Goldi was fascinated to see on her upper lip a light brown moustache. He had seen some older married women with a moustache, because they had been considered a thing of beauty, but they had always been tattooed on. This home-grown one was something else.

Their visitor looked at Goldi's ruddy but whitish skin in some surprise, then poured out her troubles in a mixture of American and Japanese. Okawa was much smaller than Goldi, but he was nearly twenty now and had quite a good grasp of the English language that was taught in some language schools, but parrot fashion. He had tried that, but also watched US TV. He honoured his father and loved his mother, but he did not want to spend all his life in a small village. In time he hoped to get to Tokyo or somewhere similar to stretch his mind more fully. After he had put Goldi in the picture he said he was not willing to take the woman out. He said however he would help provide food and other items for their journey from his house.

The weather was quite settled this season, so early the next day Miss Jenkins was ready to go off and they understood each other well enough to get by. They reached a very small island without incident. At first Goldi stayed by the boat as she started looking. She came back after a while and showed she wanted some help. A bit further round the sea had formed a small cave. She wanted to explore that, although it meant wading knee-deep to do so. There was quite a lot of flotsam about, which made her nervous, but Goldi's presence reassured her. She was then able to poke about to her heart's content in the overhanging cave face.

Goldi was almost dozing in the fairly warm sun when she called out in some excitement. He opened his eyes to see her floundering back to him with something in her hands. In her haste she tripped and went more than waist-deep into the water. He noticed she did not release her prize however. She just recovered and carried on. When she offered it for his inspection he thought it looked just like an ordinary piece of rock, but he nodded wisely, then helped her back to the boat. He started getting the food ready, while she took the bottle of saké and took a large gulp. She was he saw not used to it and it made her splutter. Goldi as usual was now enjoying his food and smiled at her. She was obviously rather excited and instead walked up and down talking to him. He could only understand a few words, but nevertheless smiled and nodded. Suddenly she threw herself down and kissed him fiercely on the lips. He was amazed, because his people just nibbled at each other to show desire or affection. The feel of her soft moustache was another first for him. Soon she struggled out of the still damp trousers and they made love violently.

With Fugi it was a long, leisurely affair, but with this strange, rather bony woman it was explosive. Were all American women like this he wondered? When she had just about worn herself out she turned away from him, crying. This upset him and he tried to comfort her, but then she was like a wildcat, so he left her alone. Eventually she quietened down, put her trousers back on and splashed her face with seawater. She took her portion of food and they finished that in silence. She squeezed his hand then before tidying everything up. On the way back in the boat she inspected the things in the box and by the time they got back to the village she was her normal self.

When Miss Jenkins finally left, Okawa said, 'Did she find everything she was looking for?'

'Yes,' said Goldi pausing for thought, 'I think so.'

This odd little adventure had only taken up one day, but it left a strong impression on Goldi's mind. He began to learn as much American and Japanese as Okawa could get through to him. He felt that some time in the future he might travel and see what other peoples and places could teach him. Meanwhile the life he was leading had quite a lot to satisfy him for now.

The wedding ceremony took place with Fugi when he was twenty. There was the usual big feast with much drinking from the ceremonial bear cups and most of his village attended. After that they moved into the new hut he had made with others' help. Apart from the lovemaking they were still very much like brother and sister and got on very well. He was not able to see Okawa so often, but they still met from time to time. However, about a year and a half later Okawa left home to seek his fortune or future. Before he left he presented Goldi with a newer, improved little boat that was very stable and seaworthy for its size. This not surprisingly became a highly prized possession. A bit later he was able to buy Fugi the hibachi she had wanted. That mainly came into play in bad weather or if they had visitors. He used the boat whenever he was able. The main difference between them was she cared little what happened outside the village, but that was mainly where his mind dwelt.

During the eight years they were married they had two children. These were unfortunately both girls, but he still loved them. At the end of this time they decided to separate and then he divorced her. Officially this was because she had not borne him sons, but really they had just grown away from each other. With their race there was little formality involved in this unlike in others. She moved back to her parents taking the most valued possessions. Of course the two girls went as well.

Goldi went back to his old grandparents. He had helped enlarge the in-laws place first, so they were not overcrowded. Although split up in such a small community they were not out of touch. The old couple were glad to have his strength now as theirs faded. These days he wondered more about his real parents, but his sense of respect for the old man stopped him pushing it. He had long known his mother had died soon after his birth. Her mother said, 'She was so young and so beautiful.' From that he had gathered there was a mystery they kept close. Two years after the divorce the old man died, then three after that his grandmother. They had not accumulated many possessions, as that was not the Ainu way. However they had been respected by their people and were honoured in their deaths.

Goldi kept one or two items as mementos and divided the others among relations. He was now thirty-three, full-grown and free to do what he liked. He was not overburdened with things for the same reason as the others. He could now go and work in local mines. They paid reasonable money and produced gypsum, copper and sulphur. Many of the local men carried on about the money they earned. Goldi did not despise it, but he had managed with little except for Fugi's fancies. He could get work where they grew sugar beet or maybe even in Tokyo, but he could not imagine himself in such a busy place. He knew from experience the sea and hills could provide for most things from prawns up to whales.

He remembered when he had been about ten being

taken to visit relatives in Sapporo. It was also the time of the Snow Festival. To a village boy like himself Sapporo had seemed a very noisy, busy place. He had enjoyed all the unusual sights. The centrepiece was the snow-sculptured statue of Hotei. That Buddha-like shape represented the Japanese god of luck. He later learnt that the town was unlike most in the country, as it was laid out in straight lines – most unusual. He was not tempted to return now however. He must decide: if he stayed locally he could take another wife for his comfort without too much trouble. If he went travelling anything might crop up, good or bad. If he enquired he might be able to meet up again with Okawa, but he realised that their relationship would most likely be different, his old friend could even have a regular woman friend now. He remembered the American woman from years back, but did not know where that place was, or if they would want a country boy like him. Finally he thought to put himself in the hands of the gods and the strength of his boat.

All these thoughts were driven from his mind now. He realised he was in that boat, but it had hit the side of a bigger one. It was now very dark and that craft, like his, was travelling without any lights. Was it a Japanese one that had been out for marlin or sword-fish? He did not know or care at the moment, as he saw water was leaking into his craft. Now he shouted at the other craft which was still underway and prayed someone would hear before he was left floundering in the water.

Chapter Two

Hiro had fallen asleep when he should have been controlling the boat. As a good seaman he knew that this was a very bad failure of duty, however he had never felt so tired-out before. The old couple and the daughter had tried to help, but they were much more at home in a tailoring shop than in a big boat. He could easily have slept a solid twelve hours, but felt he must try to get to Yokohama before he could really relax.

Although he had never been to Japan he had thought about it since he was a small boy. For some reason his sailor father had jumped ship at Vladivostok. Somehow he had then made his way to Amgu which was a small port surrounded on three sides by tree-covered hills. After some while he had met and married one of two sisters and in due time become a father. There was not much choice of work in that part of Russia, but being a sailor he soon adapted to the life of a fisherman. He worked on one of the boats which was operated by the wife's family. Because of that background Hiro had grown up hearing of life in many different countries. Being a boy he saw all of these in a romantic light. His father too was something of a dreamer. His brother-in-law called him a drifter or worse, but Shiga had not let that worry him. He did not bother about too many things being fairly easy-going. The mother called her son Boris, but the father always called him Hiro. When the boy was sixteen and working on a boat his father had suddenly disappeared without leaving any message. His wife had always kept very close contact with her family and to Hiro did not seem very affected by the loss of her partner. It seemed she cared more for her parents, sister and in-laws. Hiro however had lost father, friend and that guide to other lands.

Hiro did not say much about those feelings, but made up his mind to get away as soon as a good opportunity arose. He knew that his father had come from a small place not far from Yokohama and that he aimed to reach somehow. He knew the name of his lost father's brother and hoped that what he had heard of family loyalty in Japan would be strong enough to stretch as far as a half-Russian nephew. He did not expect to find his father there, but they would give him breathing space to think of the future.

'Comrade Gromyko could you find me some work in the timber business?'

Gromyko was a big noise in the local timber business. Like everything else this was under state control, but there still had to be somebody on the spot to organise and control the work.

'Why young Boris? I thought you had enough to do fishing.'

'Well comrade now that my father has gone I feel that I ought to try to bring some more money into the home.'

Gromyko was quite a kindly old bear, even if he did make a lot of money out of shady private deals. He ruffled the boys sleek, dark hair, then said, 'I'll see what I can do.'

Shortly afterwards he had contacted Hiro and offered him some work with a relative in a private way. So it came about Hiro had two incomes: one from fishing and one from furniture-making. All this of course kept the boy very busy, so he had less time to dwell on his father's absence, family or even girls. He knew all the local children right back from his days in the state crèche. When he thought of love or romance however he always saw in his mind's eye a Japanese maid dressed in a rich kimono. She of course would be waiting just for him, her lord and master. We are fortunate if able to dream at no other cost than eventual reality, and sometimes dreams *do* come true.

Although he was slowly building up a stock of money Hiro did not see how he would be able to support himself if he did reach Japan. Charity even from a relative is a chancy commodity. When he got a bit older he heard about various Jewish people who tried to get out of Russia by all sorts of legal or illegal means. Without a word to his mother he tried to find out more. Eventually he had a contact in Khabarovsk who knew of Jews who were very keen to get away. All this had to be done very quietly. The less people who knew the less chance there was of getting caught. Because of his steady work and apparent satisfaction with life there was no reason for people to suspect Hiro of any dubious actions. His Japanese appearance mattered little, for there were many types in Russia and more so where boats called in at times.

After much preparation Hiro one summer night picked up his new passengers. It was a rainy night and a lonely spot. That was good as there were not likely to be sharp-eyed lovers around the beach.

The old man with his greying beard, his wife and his daughter did not look prosperous. However, their most important luggage was a couple of small, but heavy bags. These contained gold. This was a good arrangement for all concerned, because that metal is valued in almost every part of the world.

Hiro's boat was sturdily made with a reliable, quietish engine and a sail. He had been secretly building up a stock of fuel over many months and that was now carefully stored up for this, his longest ever trip. He had worked out plans over a long time, but still luck came into everything. His plan had been to head straight out to sea, then go round the east coast of the island of Hokkaido. This was not the quickest way to Yokohama and it took him near other territories controlled by the USSR. His reason for choosing this route was that it avoided most of the Russian shipping lanes. Those big vessels were his biggest worry.

He was not happy about leaving his mother and relations without any explanation. However, he did not think they would worry about his absence for some time. They were used to him going away for periods and he should be able to write to them at a later stage. He had given up his second job a while back saying he thought he should start enjoying himself more. His boss thought he had girls and maybe marriage in mind. Hiro had not said otherwise.

When the Jewish family scrambled aboard the old man had said, 'What do you want us to do?'

'Let us get the women settled first,' Hiro had said.

The little cabin could just about hold the four of them, but somebody had to keep the boat on course. After a while he said, 'I'll show you how to steer.' The old man was a very poor pupil, but Hiro knew he had to have some sort of break from the job. Luckily after adjusting to their situation a bit the daughter joined them. Hiro thought between the two of them he might get some rest later. The first couple of days were likely to be the most dangerous. If he could stay awake that long he might be able to take a break. Being born to the sea he had imagined everybody had some ability to handle a vessel – now he was learning differently.

When they were not otherwise occupied the old couple seemed to spend a lot of time praying. Did they really have a strong belief or was this mainly fear? He did not really know or care. At twenty-three he was an optimistic young man and forward-looking. On just one occasion he had to get the old man to help put some fishing nets over the side. This was when a fairly large vessel was rather near. He did not know if they were Russian or Japanese. That was not important. Whoever they were he did not want to answer any questions with these passengers aboard – they were too obviously different. Approaching Hokkaido and still not far from Russian territory he could not trust the boat to unskilled hands, so he kept going that bit longer. All the time he was showing almost no lights, so as not to be seen by anybody. The steady throb of the engine on a calm sea had a lulling effect on him. He was thus almost alseep when the collison occured.

'What's that?' he cried as the thud on the side of the boat brought him to his senses.

'Help, help I'm sinking!' Goldi shouted back in Japanese. Hiro looked over the starboard side and saw his small craft. It was wallowing and obviously in trouble. As soon as he could he circled back and came alongside.

'Is it a Russian?' asked the old man while the women watched.

'I do not know,' Hiro said sharply. 'All I know is he

needs our help straight away.' As the cries had been in Japanese it was not likely to be a Russian. Even if it had been, few mariners would forsake somebody readily.

Hiro went to help Goldi aboard, but before he accepted he said, 'What about my boat?' As he was now speaking in his own tongue they could not understand, but it soon became obvious to all. Now the old man's fear had abated he was interested to know what language this was he heard. From what he could see in the lantern light this face with its full beard could even be that of an orthodox Jew. He also appeared to be wearing something like a skullcap. To come across such a puzzle in the midst of their flight aroused his curiosity.

Goldi hung onto the line he had been thrown, but there was the problem of how to get the soggy small boat aboard. The surprise now was the old man almost took charge. He got the daughter to fetch a couple of pots from the little kitchen. After Goldi had got some water out the girl could also help. Then with most of the water and the belongings out they were able to get all aboard. The wife did her bit and put those things away as best she could. Goldi of course was very pleased to get all this help and with his strength it was not too long before they could all feel they had done something special. When they were underway again the family could not really understand more than a little of Goldi's talk. Goldi and Hiro did better in Japanese, but nothing elaborate. The old man would have liked to question Goldi about his religion and background, but that type of subject could only have been gone into in the Ainu tongue. The only good result of that was the old fellow had not come down on any side about the stranger.

It seemed a good time to relax a little Hiro thought. He gave everyone a shot of his vodka. Then Goldi undid a bundle and got a bottle of saké out for another shot. This eased the strain that they had all been through, then the two younger men stayed together and the family settled down. With Goldi obviously handy with sea ways the men found language flowed better now which was a help.

When Hiro said they were heading for Yokohama Goldi was quite happy at the prospect. He thought he was in the hands of the gods. This might be part of their plan for him. He asked Hiro about the boat's engine and that gave Hiro the idea that they could share the work. Had his gods smiled on a tired sailor?

The journey was a bit more carefree after this. They were now out of the path of any Russian ships, there were two proper sailors and also Goldi was a Japanese citizen. As well as helping with the craft he caught some fish which improved their diet. The weather got a bit rougher and the family suffered some sea-sickness. That was not surprising with their background. Now the men thought to call in somewhere for some fresh supplies. Fruit and fresh water would be welcome to everybody. They did not want to try any little village, because they would question strangers. An average-sized place would be occupied with their own lives. They found what they wanted at Misawa, a fairly lively place. The two men wandered around and got fresh fruit which included oranges. These were an unusual treat for them, but seemed rather dear. Obviously gold could not be used there, so Goldi's supply of money went down fairly quickly. Later the old man said he would help when there was a safe chance of changing a little gold. The family had to stay out of sight on the boat meanwhile. Hiro looked more at home here, but the odder-looking Goldi managed the language better. He was also used to spending a little yen.

The men did not have any drinks or other extras, but got back to the boat as soon as they could. They set off again in decent weather and when they reached a nice-looking beach helped the Tratski family ashore. They did not want to stop there for more than an hour. Even that was risky. If any authority-types came along they could not explain things very well. They had pleaded to feel dry land under their feet. This outing would be their only one before reaching Yokohama.

If Goldi puzzled Mr Tratski the feeling was mutual. He knew they were not Ainu by their appearance and the old lady braided her hair like a Russian. They seemed to speak Russian, but there was a difference. Hiro knew more, but his Japanese was not really wide enough to cover the Jewish history under the czars or the Reds. It was easier to drop that subject and concentrate on the more mundane like fresh food and drink.

The two younger men steered into Sendai, telling the family to keep out of sight again while they got fresh supplies with little trouble. This was their last call, then they headed out into deeper water. Up to this point the coast had been green with crops or trees. As they moved further down the sky at night was lit more by smoke and flames. These came not from some volcano, but furnaces or tall chimneys. Goldi looked at these with distaste, but Hiro was thrilled. It looked like things were happening there and he wanted to experience that at close hand. Goldi wanted change and new experiences also, but not with giant buildings or machines. He did not like the look of this for any length of time.

They had all been together on this fairly small boat

about two or three weeks now. They were quite relaxed as a party. Neither of the young men felt specially drawn sexually to the young woman, Esther. She was slightly plump, about twenty-five to thirty they thought. Maybe because of the lack on the sexual side they got on well with her. When it was quiet Goldi taught her a few of the English words he knew. Then she remembered odd bits she had heard on the radio. She seemed to have a very good memory and learnt much quicker than he ever had. He also tried to teach her how to fish, but that was a different story. It seemed odd to the men, but they could not put themselves into the mindset of ordinary town-folk. Hiro might need to learn that, while Goldi aimed to avoid it if possible. As they drew in sight of Yokohama Goldi was nervous. As Hiro was steering this last bit Goldi sought refuge in that old friend saké and was soon a bit drunk. The others did not like to see this, as he was half the crew. Mainly with Esther's help he stopped.

If Goldi could travel back two hundred years he would have seen that Yokohama then was just a decent-sized fishing town. Then an earthquake had destroyed it. It had been rebuilt after a while on a larger scale. Later all that had been destroyed again by US bombers. Again it had to be rebuilt, but now the harbour was made much deeper to take the ever-larger boats. Some of the silt was used to build up swampy bits and factories could then be put up on this new land. Japan, like Holland, did not have much spare space, so this was worthwhile.

Once they got into this place they knew they would have to deal with immigration people and maybe police. The Tratskis hoped to get to America or Britain if all went well. They agreed Goldi could come along if he wished. Hiro wanted to stay in Japan at least for the time being. Goldi had all that explained to him and was quite happy to fit in with their ideas.

They had to steer very carefully now, as there were so many craft around. These ranged from a few matting-sailed fishing boats, then through different types of goods and passengers coasters right up to the largest ships which called in at San Francisco and other American ports. Despite all the bustle and movement their arrival had not gone unnoticed.

As they looked for somewhere to tie up safely they saw two policemen on the quay in an open jeep. One of these waved towards some steps and when Hiro drew alongside jumped nimbly aboard. He then rattled out a string of questions to Hiro. Hiro shook his head and turned towards Goldi for help. This was a big surprise to the cop. He was slightly acquainted with some Ainu, but those he had seen were fairly short and he thought seemed backward. This man looked from a different mould. He had their normal-style skin clothes, but was taller and maybe a bit lighter. Now Goldi asked the man what he wanted in slow, careful Japanese.

The policeman now spoke the same way. What were they all doing in a Russian-type fishing boat? Who was the old bearded man and family? How was it that Hiro looked Japanese, but could not understand the language? Why was there another smaller boat aboard?

Goldi did his best with this lot, but it obviously was not good enough for a Japanese law-enforcer. He called across to his mate, then got them to move the boat under his direction. Hiro finally moored it by a quiet, fenced-in section of the harbour.

They all disembarked and were led to a low wooden building. Goldi thought all this questioning and police activity rather strange, but if the others were not both-ered he was not going to make a fuss. He knew that if he wished he could explain about himself and return to Hokkaido, but return to do what? He would much rather stay with his fellow travellers and see what happened.

The next day a Japanese who could speak Russian came along. After quite a long while he got the full story from the Tratskis and Hiro. He made a lot of notes, then went off. The next day Goldi was told he had been checked up and was 'in the clear'. He was free to go anywhere now within reason. He thanked them, but said he would like to stay with the others and also work on getting his boat back in shape. After more discussion this was agreed to. With Hiro he explained he needed to get it up somewhere solid before starting. The policemen said okay and even helped with that. He told them he had money for the job and they let a craftsman come in to help.

It was not long before his little prize was good as new. Goldi had no wish to explore the big, noisy town. He just wanted to get onto the water again. In the harbour there was no wind for the sail, but he could use oars or paddle. When he first went near some of the larger boats some sailors laughed at this oddity. A few threw coins his way and some more unpleasant things. He did not show his annoyance at that, but moved away and after kept a thick fur hat near to hand. He did not want to get a dented skull. He of course always had to keep his eyes open for bigger, faster ships moving about. It did not take long to know their ways.

Hiro said it would be some days before the necessary papers were ready for them all. Goldi had seen how police and officials were always writing something or other. Maybe that was all these town people could do? How did they get their food and fuel for fires etc.? He could have taught them to make sails and catch fish to live, but a town would have to be nearly all beach for that. All of them had a futon to sleep on in a dry hut, but after a couple of meals they had to pay for their food. There were plenty of places near for that and Goldi did not mind just that little venture out.

He could have caught fish nearby, but these waters were full of all types of filth. On his coast the weather and conditions were often rough, but the water was clean and the fish also. Mr Tratski was quite happy to pay for any items these days. He was very grateful to Hiro and also Goldi for their help in getting him and the family here safely and he was not a mean man. Goldi wondered how he could find enough money if the family tried to get as far as America. He found part of the answer near at hand.

When Goldi was moving round the harbour he often saw groups of schoolchildren with their teachers. All were neatly dressed in blue. The boys had short haircuts and the girls often had plaits. They did what they were told by the teachers, but made quite a lot of noise otherwise. Many of the teachers pointed out the odd bearded boatman as one of the sights of the harbour. On two occasions he took each child in the group on a short trip and was well paid for that. One day two teachers signalled for him to come over and talk. He knew they had brought their classes here before. He was very surprised to eventually realise they wanted to buy his boat for the school. After a lot of discussion they offered Goldi what seemed a great deal of money. He wanted to refuse, but asked them to come back in an hour or so. He then spoke to Mr Tratski and said how much would a trip to the US cost? He did not mention his boat. Mr Tratski had enquired and gave him a figure. This was more than his boat would fetch, but was well on the way. Feeling a bit unhappy he met the teachers as arranged. He cheered up when he found they had also been talking and now had raised their offer quite a bit. He agreed to this then. Now if he did go that far with the Tratskis he would still have a little money left. Until the last couple of weeks he had never bothered much about money. Having to part with his boat brought home the importance of it in this new world he found himself exploring, so different from his fishing village and ways.

Chapter Three

Yokohama had once been the centre of a thriving passenger-boat service, berthing as it did the largest of ocean-going liners. Their heyday had passed now however. This was because the majority of travellers preferred the speed and comfort that they could now find in the liners of the sky. One thing the Americans shared with their oriental rivals was a strong sense of urgency and competitive ways.

The Japanese still retained their traditional type of theatre and tea ceremonies. Otherwise they thought that in life the prizes went to the swiftest. When our group enquired about passage to America they were advised to go by jet aircraft. Apart from Esther they were not brave enough to even consider that ordeal. Apart from various freighters which went from one Japanese island to another there was still one shipping line that sailed to San Francisco. It was the fare for that Mr Tratski had quoted.

Goldi and his boat had not been parted straight away. One delay was arranging something to move it without any damage. The other had been his ignorance of large money-handling. The school had offered him a cheque or large currency notes. As he had not handled either he was very doubtful. Both of these bits of paper did not seem the things to pay for all that travel. In the end Goldi went with the two teachers he knew to a large bank. There they had arranged to meet the chief cashier. They were shown into his office which was away from all the other hubbub. There a grey-haired man gravely assured him all would be well and above board. If Goldi would take a cheque it would be easier to look after and quite safe. Soon after that was settled they found out papers had come through so that they could at least visit America. Hiro was told he could visit his uncle as well.

Now they had got that far Mr Tratski said to Goldi, 'Do not worry about the money for the trip, it can be settled later.'

Goldi said, 'Thank you very much, but I have the money.'

As they had all been confined to the small area all this time they had not realised all the things Goldi had been up to. When Goldi finally managed to get across all the details of the children, the school and the two teachers the others were very quiet for a while. Then Esther came close and gave him a kiss. Like the others she knew how much that boat had meant to him. Then Mr Tratski came and kissed him on both cheeks.

Goldi now looked nervously at Mrs Tratski, but he was safe there. She just nodded her head a few times and smiled. Finally they had to say their goodbyes to Hiro. This was a sad time for Goldi. He had got on very well with the younger fisherman. They had made a good team on the tricky voyage and he would miss him. The Tratski relationship with Hiro had originally been just businesslike, but with their shared experiences at sea a real bond had been established. He got the agreed share of money Mr Tratski had promised plus a helpful bonus. Being a young man Hiro mainly looked forward. He had received a friendly message from his uncle and now with the money in his pocket he had good reason to be optimistic. Nevertheless later he would realise that the trip had widened his interest in people outside Japan. He took the name and details of a Jewish agency Mr Tratski told of in New York. Through that he would be able to get in touch with them later if he wished.

Now that everything was settled the others were keen to get started for the US. Luckily their boat was due to sail in two days' time. One of the people from immigration helped with that and other arrangements. Ships often sailed half-empty except for some goods, so they got places on board to suit all. However, on the day of embarkation they all suffered from nerves. Goldi had a few drinks hoping that would help. Momma and Poppa Tratski (as he thought of them these days) were on the quiet side. He saw them quietly praying once. Esther was the least worried and her organising way helped make up a bit for Hiro's departure. The size of the ship was intimidating. They all stayed on deck to see the gangways removed, ropes cast off then the view of the port and Japan get smaller and smaller. Once clear of the rather foggy harbour the wind picked up, so they made their way below decks.

Goldi thought the mattress on his bed was too soft. He stripped off the bedclothes, put the mattress outside and made up the bed roughly. He dozed off, but there was a knock on the door he had left half-open. A brown face over a white collar stared in.

'This your mattress out here man?'

'Yes, I like a hard futon.'

The steward studied the big, bearded white man in the strange gear. Was this guy having him on? The man might have been a rich eccentric, but that was not likely as this was not a top-class cabin.

'Okay I'll take it away this time,' he said.

Just as well thought Goldi. If he hadn't I might have thrown it over the side. He was not too happy being stuck inside this large vessel. After some time he began to realise how much space there was in the ship. It was certainly bigger than his old village. After he had dozed some more he decided he had better go up on deck to ease his bladder. First he went into the corridor. He looked at the many doors, some with writing on them which meant nothing to him. He climbed a couple of sets of stairs without meeting anybody and then was outside. He went to the rail and started urinating which was a relief. Suddenly he heard a scream and when he turned round saw a meaty woman with blue/grey hair. She then screamed again even louder. She clutched at the arm of a smallish, balding man who looked rather flustered.

'Elmer look at that filthy beast! Are you going to let him insult me like this?' Elmer tried to say something soothing to her.

While Goldi was wondering what all the fuss was about one or two more people had appeared. One of these was the brown steward.

'Can I help you sir?' he said to Elmer. The little man then muttered in his ear and handed over some money.

'That's all right sir, leave it to me,' the steward said. He then came over to Goldi and said, 'Will you come along with me and I'll show you where everything is?'

After hearing that woman scream Goldi did not argue this time. 'I don't know what kind of nut I've got here, but I'd better start from square one,' thought Sam, the steward.

They went down to Goldi's deck and Sam stopped outside a door not far from his cabin. 'This is the toilet, bathroom or john.' Goldi tried to explain he had seen the picture of a man, but he was not doing anything.

'If we showed all that we would be in more trouble than *you!*' Inside he showed the shower, sink and all the rest. This took quite a while, but Sam thought if it stopped any more scenes it would be worthwhile. Goldi's head was clear by now and he realised that this man was doing what he could to help. He had always gone over the side of his boat or in bushes if away from anywhere, but now he would try to follow the American way. Did these people train their dogs to perform like this? Some big hounds would make as much mess as a man.

Goldi certainly did not want old women screaming at him, so he decided he had better do what this man had told him. He went back to his cabin rather quietly while Sam went off, shaking his head.

Being town-folk the Tratskis did not have that type of problem and Esther was able to help with the few that did. There were a number of Japanese on board, a few Australians, more Americans and others, so they were a mixed lot. The cooks tried to cater for most tastes without going for luxury. This means sweetcorn, some dried fish, rice, seaweed, other seafoods and burgers. Goldi enjoyed these meals and tucked in with his knife while the Americans used forks and the Japanese chopsticks.

Our travellers settled into routines that passed the time easily enough, but there were a couple of incidents. Poppa Tratski with his beard, dark clothes and Russian-type speech stood out a bit from most who chose light, brighter clothes. One afternoon a group of American teenagers, having exhausted the limited amusements the ship provided, were bored. When they came upon this old fellow in a quiet part of the ship they hung about and made jokes at his expense. One or two nastier ones even touched his beard or hat. Mr Tratski was not over-worried, as Russians could also be crude.

Goldi had enjoyed his food and also some drink. He knew the old fellow liked it quiet at times, but decided to try to find him. Coming round a corner and seeing this happen he let out a roar and seized two youths. He then dangled them over the rail. The rest of the group were shocked into silence by this, but Mr Tratski came forward and got Goldi to stop. Still very angry Goldi shook them before letting them go off. The rest also had had enough. There were some benefits from this. One was that Goldi could not be looked on as a joke, but had to be watched now. There were also no more incidents for the Tratskis. Surprisingly there were no comebacks from the youths' parents. Mothers can be a tough lot, but it seemed the lads did not want to be asked what had started off all this fuss, as they would look bad.

There were deck games in the day and some music at night, but none of our group joined in these. Esther spent a lot of time in the smallish library reading English. She realised the better she got at it the more help she would be to all in the US or even in England. The old lady was content as long as her husband and daughter were okay.

They had not really suffered in Russia and Mrs Tratski was sorry in some ways to have left the life she knew. For the sake of her only daughter's future if for nothing else she was content to go along with them and help if she could.

Halfway through the trip the captain ran a carnival day. Some extra drink was supplied, decorations were put up and the passengers were encouraged to entertain each other. Some of the youngsters made up a beat group, an American matron offered to sing, while three Australians offered to sing choruses if they got enough beer. The captain approached Goldi and said he had heard he was a good wrestler. Goldi denied this, but was eventually persuaded to have a go to entertain the others. An offer of a nice lot of free vodka helped to change his mind.

Luckily carnival day turned out calm and sunny. Everything then could take place on an open part of the deck. Everybody came along. Few people can resist seeing their neighbours acting the fool. One of the ship's officers was the master of ceremonies. The beat group were first and slaughtered some well-known numbers. Younger ones shouted for *more*. The MOC agreed to a couple, then it was the turn of the lady singer who had the stage. She turned out to sound like that rich lady who used to hire the Carnegie Hall, but her timing was worse. The next item was the wrestling match. Goldi was stripped to the waist and wore a tough pair of skin trousers. Sam was acting as his second and had covered Goldi with a liberal coating of grease. His opponent was a stocky Japanese in a judo suit. He was wearing a green belt. This indicated he was not a high grade, but had learnt the fundamentals and got up a few rungs. The contest started with the striking of a dinner gong. There were no elaborate rules except no punching or head-butting. Also for Goldi's benefit no hair-pulling was allowed either. At the first gong the judo man knelt and touched the stretched canvas with his forehead. Goldi, full of enthusiasm and a little vodka rushed over and sent his opponent sprawling. The few Japanese men present had to be stopped from attacking Goldi over this. The referee, rather shaken, stopped everybody and a fresh start was made. This time there was no bowing or rushing. The two men approached each other with arms outstretched. The Japanese tried a stomach throw, but failed. To do that in judo one normally grasps the other person's canvas coat at chest height, rolls backwards with a foot to the stomach, then lets go. Goldi's greasy torso gave him no purchase. He finished up gasping with his opponent's full weight on top of him. Goldi was now in a good position to apply an arm-lock or use the man's coat to choke him, but because of his lack of skill did neither. The referee got them up again and awarded Goldi a point. The Japanese now abandoned normal judo. After moving round so as to be out of sight of the referee he elbowed Goldi very hard in the belly. He gasped and sat down heavily on the canvas. Immediately the Japanese slipped round behind him and applied a stranglehold. Seeing Goldi's face turning blue the referee broke them up, awarded the oriental a point and the first round ended.

When the gong went for the second Goldi, now very sober, came forward cautiously. They circled for a time, then the Japanese caught hold of a wrist and ducking under the arm threw Goldi to the canvas. That gave his opponent another point. Winded Goldi stayed on his knees for a while until sent to his corner. There, looking very worn, he thought out a plan. As soon as the gong sounded he managed to rush his opponent and swing him off his feet. He then staggered across the deck and managed to drop the furious man into the small swimming pool. This last effort was really too much for him and he also fell into the water. The referee decided that was enough and said the match had been a draw. This bout had certainly given all the spectators their entertainment. When the two men had recovered a bit Goldi went over and shook hands. The

Japanese man did not bear Goldi any malice now. Like most of his race he respected a tough opponent. As they went off to clean up the three Australians who were now lubricated enough led a general sing-song which ended the entertainment. The captain finished off his carnival by presenting small gifts to the participants. He added extra praise and presents of their favourite tipple to the two former fighters.

The rest of the trip was quiet for the Tratskis, but Goldi managed another incident. Sam had kept a fairly close eye on him since the outraged matron. He saw the cabin door was left ajar and told Goldi of it. He however did not like being shut in down there. Once, feeling very hot, he decided to sleep on deck. One of the crew passing saw his door open, but nobody inside. He checked later and finding it still empty told an officer and a search was ordered. That man did not disturb the old couple, but woke Esther. Startled she said she had not seen Goldi since the evening. She was anxious for him, but annoyed that they had woken her. Did they think Goldi would be in with her? Anyhow, she would have to help look for this big idiot! She put on a few clothes and joined the sailors. After about half an hour of looking somebody said he might have drunk too much and fallen overboard. Esther doubted that, knowing his experience of drink and the sea. Eventually it was she who found him fast asleep on top of a life-raft. In her relief and annoyance she stormed at him violently. Goldi had never seen this side of her before and he did not enjoy it. After this he slept in the cabin with the door shut. It was not nice, but he got used to it.

In the mainly quiet times Esther got to know one of the junior officers and practised her English on him. As there was no kind of romance going on Goldi sometimes joined them. He picked up more words and was also able to look at parts of the ship's equipment. He did not touch anything without permission – he could do without any more scenes. He was however more curious about things than most Ainu. These people are the only whites in an area dominated by Asiatics. The Japanese called them the 'hairy ones' because many liked to grow thick beards. The winters in their area were mainly very cold, so that was not very surprising. Japanese and Mongolian types seldom grow much facial or body hair. The Ainu race were getting rather diluted as they intermarried with others. They were most numerous in the Kuril Islands which were under the control of the USSR which did not please the Japanese powers. An unusual feature of the pure members is a protruding forehead. That made the nose appear to be in a recess. Goldi knew he was not like that and it made him wonder all the more at times about his father. Anyhow he was able to look at equipment that meant little to him. He also had a look in the big engine room. That was very impressive, but he did not like the noise or smell.

Momma and Poppa Tratski had been through many experiences in their lives. It was strange to be so far out on the sea without fellow Jews or Russians, but they were not very bothered. As Esther was so adaptable she could help them with most things. She worried a bit about their future, but did not show or say anything. After breakfast one day they were told they could soon have a view of San Francisco, God and fog willing. That caused a buzz of excitement among those who had never seen the place before. At lunchtime they were in sight and the weather was fine. The first thing they saw was a line of mountains, then nearer other features stood out. They could see the town was on a peninsula.

To reach it they had first to go through a waterway that was bordered on their left hand by green hills. Then they were in a large harbour which was set in an elliptical-shaped saucer. All this was surrounded by mountains. Fens, plains and deserts all have their appeal, but most people get a thrill from the contrast between steep hills and large lakes or harbours. This well-watered and fertile area was one of the more impressive.

They passed under a bridge which someone said was called 'The Golden Gate'. The ship then headed for the town on their right. Like Yokohama the port was busy with all types of shipping and small craft, but there were no sampans here Goldi could see. When a small but powerful boat came quite near he asked what it was used for. 'Tuna fishing I think,' said his neighbour. Goldi did not comment, but he was surprised. In Japan that was quite a serious affair. A good-sized boat went out and when they were in the right area up to twenty men stood on special boards outside the hull. Each of these men would be equipped with a stout rod and line. As they hooked a tuna the fishermen would throw it backwards over their heads into the main body of the boat. There other men or boys would unhook these, rebait the the line and then the procedure would start all over again. Normally the boat would return to port with a full load. That would then be transferred to the shore where women were waiting to prepare the fish for the canning process. In Japan most fishing was either big business or else, like Goldi's, mainly to feed a family. Here in America it looked like a game for rich boys.

When they docked somebody pointed out an area called downtown. How was that different from San Francisco? They would find out. People started moving away from the rail, getting ready to disembark. However, Goldi, the family and a few others had to wait and they sat with their few belongings in one of the lounges. Now they had actually reached America they were all feeling a bit nervous. Goldi and these Russian Jews had no family waiting for them. The two younger ones had the best grasp of English, but it was still sketchy. There had been Americans on this ship, but were they like most or were there gangsters who ran the country in partnership with big business? There had been stories of poor white people as well as negroes who suffered from malnutrition. This was meant to be happening in the richest country in the world. This was what the Tratskis has seen many times on Russian TV and in films. They had seen films made from the stories of Jack London who was an American and they were also generally bleak. However, they had been quite well treated on this ship apart from that odd incident, so maybe they did not have too much to worry about. In the end all they could do was to pray to the God of their fathers and wait as patiently as possible.

Goldi did not have the Tratski worries, as he had seen very little propaganda of any sort. He did though feel more alone than that family. He was sure no Ainu people had travelled here like him, so any relations he had were left far behind. He was only suited to earn a living by fishing or growing crops and from what he had seen there was not much room for that over here. But it was no good worrying and it had been his choice to come. The gods would provide something – he hoped.

Most of the passengers were up ready to go ashore, but Esther's officer friend had told them to wait and they would get sorted out. They all needed that tricky thing now – patience.

Chapter Four

'What have we got here then?'

When the little group reached the quayside they showed the official the papers they had been given in Yokohama. Instead of giving them a quickish look and waving them through as he had earlier people he had called over a colleague.

The two men stood together for quite a while looking at the papers and making remarks that meant nothing to our group. After some while the first man said, 'See here these papers are not much use to us. If you were just bona fide holidaymakers they would be okay, but you are not that. Where is all your gear and where are you booked to stay?'

Although Esther and Goldi had improved their English all this was too much for them to handle. Goldi felt annoyed by this extra delay after all the travelling he had done.

'See here I am from Japan and I have the papers.'

'Oh yeah,' said the official, responding to the tone in Goldi's voice. 'And where are the papers to prove you are fit and well enough to enter the United States?'

'I'll show you how fit I am.' He started to move towards the official. However Esther's hand placed firmly on his arm soon stopped that. The official had however taken a step back and now called out, 'Hey

39

Frank, I think we had better call a wagon over and take this lot to the main block. They can sort them out properly, especially the big fella.'

So they found themselves being driven off to a separate part of the docks. Goldi was to have much less freedom here though. The only way in and out was through a tough-looking locked gate. There was a uniformed guard and he did not operate his button until he was really sure about the people. All our travellers now saw that in every big place bits of paper or passes controlled so much of life. In the smaller places, even in Russia, there was far less unless you upset 'a big shot'.

Luckily, after things quietened down they were not kept inside a building all the time. Goldi could not get to the water, but he could at least see it through a high fence. With an effort he could even see parts of the town. Very politely he asked one person the names and found the high part was called Telegraph Hill.

There was a busy road bridge that led to somewhere called Oaklands. Out that way was a naval station that belonged to the armed services and an airport where one could get a plane to Europe or even back to Japan. Goldi could see helicopters landing and taking off fairly close, so knew special facilities were provided for them.

When they first got to this place they were given a meal. It was not what they would have chosen, but they did not complain. It was fried meat in a roll with a little salad. They were given the choice of coffee or Coke. Esther bravely asked for just water. They were shown where they could collect that themselves, chilled from a machine. The old couple only pecked at their food, but Esther and Goldi had better appetites. For sleeping Esther and her mother were taken one way and Goldi and the old man another. There were only narrow iron beds with thin mattresses, but that suited them and Goldi soon slept. Not so the old man who had slept alongside his wife for thirty years and found it hard to do otherwise. After a long time however he said a quiet prayer and followed Goldi's example.

In the morning they were taken to the showers and then ate an American breakfast, or some of it. After this they were left alone for an hour or so. Momma Tratski had also found it hard to get off to sleep, but Esther had pulled her bed near and reassured her. That helped the old girl get off, but Esther was awake for about an hour. She thought that now the most important step was for her to contact New York. She did not know where that was or much else, but had been given an address of a Jewish organisation. At about eleven o'clock they were shown into a large office. Three men sat at a table and a girl to one side. Nobody wore uniform and they seemed relaxed. They were pleasantly surprised when the man on the left addressed them in fluent Russian, just Goldi felt left out. This man said that many things had to be looked at before it was decided if they could stay in the US. He could help answer any questions they had. Esther took that as her cue to ask about the Jewish organisation. After speaking to the man next to him their man said that was a very useful contact. Many Jews from Russia had been helped by them in the past. Meanwhile they would all have to have medicals which included blood tests and X-rays. Goldi saw the others looked unhappy. Although they were told this would not be painful they did not like the idea of being looked all over by foreign doctors.

The Russian-speaking man now spoke directly to Goldi who only understood the odd word. The man on

41

the other side then tried talking to Goldi in slow, formal Japanese. He asked how Goldi had managed to be with these others. Goldi tried to explain about the collision and his family left behind, but it was much too complicated. Esther saw how he was struggling and tried to help, but she did not know all that much about his past either. After this the three men put their heads together and began discussing things in low tones. It was obvious they were all puzzled by this strangely dressed, fair-skinned, burly, bearded stranger. They did not say much more to our group who were then shown back to their quarters.

When lunchtime came round the Tratskis were pleased to see the food, if not Russian-style, was at least Jewish. Goldi quite enjoyed sampling plenty of bits of pickled herring and the like. In the afternoon they were all driven off in a van with an escort. They arrived at a large medical centre on the edge of town. The men were taken to their section and the women were looked at by all female staff. They were weighed, measured, tapped with hammers and generally checked over. Goldi thought all this was nonsense and wondered how he had managed to stay fit into his thirties with none of this. In his old village he had received a few simple remedies that had been passed down through generations of the wiser old ladies. The old man had been treated a number of times by a doctor back home in Khabarovsk, so took it as routine. Before any X-ray plates were made they were shown some to give them an idea of what and why. These really surprised Goldi. He thought that was how a pig looked when it was being butchered and skinned. Was this a type of magic? It must be for living lightly clothed people to look so.

He was very quiet when a youngish woman positioned him so that they could take the picture. He was almost disappointed when they said it was all done and he had felt nothing. She patted his shoulder as if he was a boy, then indicated he should take his things and get dressed again. Mr Tratski and he were then shown into a section where a sample of their blood would be taken. This made him think how his people were strengthened by the blood of the bear. This made his stomach move with unease. It was not pain he feared, but that his blood should pour out for strangers. Would that make him their slave? The old man did not look worried like him. Still bothered Goldi followed him into the room. Inside was a small black man dressed in a white coat. Also there was a meaty, white nurse. The man smiled at them and said, 'Don't worry we won't eat you!'

That was something anyhow, thought Goldi. They were helped to roll up their sleeves, then the nurse wiped their arms with damp cotton wool. The man studied their faces for a minute, then came up to Poppa Tratski with a tube that had a needle on the end. 'I'll just take a small sample,' he said, then carefully inserted the needle into the old man's arm. Just a couple of minutes and the job was done. This made Goldi rather ashamed of his fears. Following that good example he made no fuss when it was his turn. He even managed a weak smile at the girl as it was done. After this they got properly dressed and rejoined the women. Then it was back to the harbour.

After breakfast the next day Goldi was taken off on his own. Although still in the same block this room did not look pleasant. It was rather bare and windowless. A strange man sat at a desk, while to one side stood the Japanese-speaking one. Both of them had their sleeves rolled up, but wore ties. Goldi stood looking at them in silence. A voice behind him suddenly shouted out in Russian. Goldi spun round to see that speaking man looking at him quizzically. Again there was silence for a few minutes.

Then the man at the desk said, 'That's okay Stan we won't be needing you.'

Stan let himself quietly out and Goldi was motioned to a chair.

'Please what was that about?' he said.

'Oh nothing much,' said the man behind the desk. 'We thought you might understand him better than us, but it does seem we were wrong.'

Goldi thought this was peculiar, as it must have been obvious before that he could not follow the Russian speech. However, he let the matter drop.

The men behind the desk now almost smiled, and one said, 'My name is Ralph Marshall and this is Jim Sento, what's yours?'

'Goldi.'

'Just Goldi?'

'Yes, Goldi from Omu.'

'And where is that?'

'Hokkaido.'

'Japan?'

'Yes, at the top, north Japan.'

'How come you speak English?'

'How come?'

Sento then explained in careful Japanese. Goldi thought about Miss Jenkins and also Hiro. He did not feel he could go into all that. The two men exchanged glances at his silence.

'I met an English-speaking woman and my Japanese friend also did.'

Marshall said, 'Why did you try to learn English?'

Sento then said, 'Who are your people, as you are not proper Japanese?'

Goldi said, 'Do you come from Japan?'

'No, but my father did.'

'The Ainu once lived over most of Japan. Mount Fujiama was named by my people.'

Sento was surprised to hear all this and translated it to Marshall.

'Do some of your people live in Russia?'

Goldi said, 'I'm not sure, but my grandfather said something about their people living in other scattered parts.'

Sento had wandered behind Goldi and now hissed in his ear. 'Why were you asking about the naval airbase here?'

Goldi thought for a moment. Had he asked or had that man just told him? 'No reason, I just wanted to know about everything.'

Then Sento said, 'Why did you attack the immigration man?'

Goldi said, 'I did not attack him, I was . . .' How could he explain that the man had annoyed him and he wanted to show off his strength? He just shrugged his shoulders this time.

Marshall now said, 'I'm sorry Mr Goldi, but your answers are not very clear. Also we are not too sure of your papers of identity. We will have to speak to you again.' Goldi was then shown back to his quarters and told not to go outside.

Goldi rejoined his friends in a very disturbed state of mind. He tried to explain it all to Esther. She said not to worry and it was not very important. That helped him a bit, but he did not like the way these Americans treated him. He had thought of Americans as friends,

45

but now he was not so sure. The rest of the day dragged for him. Once he tried to go outside, but was stopped by a guard.

After their evening meal Goldi was escorted back to the bare room. Then he was left on his own for quite some time. At last his two questioners came in and repeated everything again. He did not have anything else to add, so they were not pleased. They next asked him about the Ainu people. He could answer that all right and as he did so they both consulted a big book in front of them. This described the bear ceremony: how the cub was trapped, raised by the mother as kindly as her own children. Goldi could talk well about that, although he had never seen it all. They asked what was the final end of the bear? Goldi told how the foster-mother would at that stage weep for her bear and then the gory manner of its death. If he had ever gone into a Roman Catholic church he could have seen the gory figure of Jesus hanging from a large cross. Maybe that image would not seem all that different to some. All his account took quite a long while, as he often searched for the right word to get the meaning across.

When he had finished the men looked more pleased. Marshall said, 'Thank you Mr Goldi you have done very well at last in answering. We think you deserve a reward. If you will follow Mr Sento he will show you what.' Puzzled Goldi obeyed and then they stood outside a brightly painted door. Sento knocked before opening it. Smiling he said, 'If there is anything else you require, just press the bell inside and I will come.'

Goldi saw the warmly lit room was furnished in Japanese style. Standing by some cushions was an attractive young girl who was dressed in traditional Japanese clothes. She came forward.

'Hello, my name is Okichi. I have been told to do whatever you wish.'

Goldi was speechless. He had never had much to do with young Japanese girls. He was not bothered by them however. When he knew Okawa he had got to know his mother and father quite well.

The girl then said, 'Would you like some food? You must be a bit hungry by now.'

That was a sensible enough question, so Goldi said yes. The girl moved aside a screen to show a long, low table with many Japanese delicacies on it. There also looked to be a very good supply of hot or cold saké plus rice beer. Goldi had not seen such a spread even back in Japan and he set to with a will. Okichi passed him whatever he needed. She ate a little and made some small talk. When they had eaten their fill she took a flask of saké, two small cups and moved across the room where padded mats lay on the floor.

'Come,' said Okichi. 'Lie down.' When Goldi hesitated she smiled and said, 'It's all right, I will give you a massage.'

Somewhat reluctantly he obeyed, but when she started he admitted she knew her job. This part of the room was dimly lit and restful. Soon he felt really soothed. She stopped then and lay down by him.

'Is there anything you would like to talk about?' she murmured.

'Mmm?' was his only reply.

'Is there anything you would really like?' she persisted.

He woke up a bit and said, 'Yes there is.'

'What is that?'

'I would love to get another boat like the one I sold back in Yokohama. Yes it was wonderful. You could sail and sail and sail,' he said as his voice petered out into a snore.

The girl was silent for a moment, then she said, 'Oh my God!' This showed that despite appearances she might be good and religious at heart.

The next morning Goldi woke up to find himself in this strange room. What had happened? he thought. Slowly it all came back to him and he lay there feeling confused. Never mind, he had enjoyed a good meal. There was no sign of the girl, but he did not miss her. He had not fancied Japanese girls much even when he was young. He felt it must be getting late and he definitely wanted some breakfast. He crossed over to the bellpush and rang, but nobody came. He waited, then tried the door. It was open and there was nobody in sight. He went on and found their area okay.

After he found the Tratskis Esther asked him what had happened. She knew he had been missing all night as her father had told them. After he managed to explain it all she looked rather amused. She then told her parents. That caused a lot of animated discussion. Finally even that stopped.

The next thing that came up was the result of their medicals. That was resolved after they had eaten their lunch. They were taken to an office, then when settled Stan the Russian-speaking man came in. He then translated the words of two strange men who were with him. One called Morgan spoke most. He said, 'I have both good and bad news for you all. First the bad. I have to say the X-ray of Mrs Tratski was not satisfactory. There is a shadow on your lung. That means you cannot stay permanently in the United States.'

This had to be translated and explained at length before they all understood it.

Morgan continued, 'We have satisfied ourselves about Mr Goldi, but unfortunately it would appear that he will have neither friends nor relatives here who could support him. Have you any other occupation or income that has not been mentioned?'

This took even longer to get across. Goldi then told Mr Morgan that all he really knew was fishing and hunting. He would have just a little money left otherwise.

Morgan then said, 'Now for the good news. This other gent here is Mr Levi. He represents The All Jewry Aid Society. I think what he has to tell you will cheer you all up a bit. I introduce Mr Levi.'

Goldi thought this Levi looked a very different type of Jew to Mr Tratski, he looked more like a fighter.

Now he raised his arms above his head and said, 'Friends I welcome you to freedom. Our Society was formed to help any Jew in need. But even more those fleeing from the bullies of Moscow.' Here he paused for dramatic effect. That was lessened by Goldi loudly whispering to Esther, 'Why does he wave his arms about?' She shushed him into silence, then Mr Levi continued.

'We know only too well what you have suffered at their hands and there is a multitude here and in Europe who weep for you and yours.'

This was a bit much for Mr Tratski. He was glad to have reached America in one piece, but it had not seemed like the Promised Land. He also had some love left for Russia.

'Excuse me interrupting your good news Mr Levi, but would you mind answering an old man's questions?'

When that had been translated Mr Levi shook his head.

'Were you born in Russia and maybe came here not long ago?'

'No, no, I am from Rhode Island USA. I have never been to Russia, but I keep up with all the latest. Does that answer your question?'

'Yes thank you, please go on.'

After a moment Mr Levi did, but in a lower key. 'Unfortunately we know you cannot stay in the USA because of Mrs Traski's X-ray.'

Here he was interrupted by Stan. 'Eh, what is that? Oh pardon me – Mrs Tratski. No I was not talking to you. I just got your name a bit wrong, that's all.'

All this had to be translated and explained before he could carry on. He did that after wiping his hands on a large handkerchief.

'However, our organisation has many friends in England. Our New York office is almost certain that you will be able to go there. If you want to it would be on a permanent basis.'

When this had been discussed and generally pulled around the Tratskis were agreed. Then they had a talk to Goldi. Meanwhile the three top men were enjoying a coffee. If possible they wanted to get all this sorted out quickly.

Esther now spoke for the group. 'We are grateful for this offer although we do not know anybody in England. Also does this include our friend Goldi? We are quite happy to pay his fare.'

Mr Levi now started asking his two companions questions.

Was this Mr Goldi a Jew?

No he did not seem to be.

Was he a Christian?

50

No, not that either.

Well what did he worship if anything?

A bear it seems and maybe ancestors.

A *bear*!

This was a problem for all three men, but the Tratskis obviously wanted Goldi to go with them. In the end they agreed that if they made sure the Tratskis would be responsible for Goldi he should be treated as a relative as far as the UK was concerned.

'Yes Miss Tratski, we will do our best to see that Mr Goldi can go along with you.'

The Tratskis had all realised that if Goldi had not fallen into their path that night there was a good chance they might not have had the choice that had been given them here and also in Japan.

When they went back to their quarters and Mr Levi had left Morgan came out with a joke about him, 'I hope Levi never attends a poultry conference.'

'Why is that?'

'Because if they started discussing Rhode Island Reds he might just run amok!'

Chapter Five

Now that it was agreed they would all go to England they had to look into ways and means. Goldi had only a small amount of his original money left. The others insisted they pay for him as they had intended if they had headed for New York. Really he had little choice. He had no boat to sell now and he was not welcome here without cash. Having done the best he could he now smiled, thanked them and tried to put all that to the back of his mind. They now all faced the travel problem together.

Will we be able to go to England by boat, Goldi had asked.

It was explained they had to cross the US before the sea crossing. Local advice was that they should fly.

The idea of that terrified Goldi. 'Why should we fly?'

It was explained that so many people flew there were far less road or rail crossings in the US than in Europe. Even the old river boats were only a tourist showpiece these days.

'What is a paddleboat?' asked Goldi, really interested.

'No don't bother, that was a joke.'

In the end they were all persuaded this was really the best way, but none of them were happy with that prospect.

Once the immigration people were satisfied Goldi was an ingenuous traveller from North Japan and not a fellow traveller of the enemy they were more amiable. They were also relieved that future problems with him were for the Tratskis, not them.

While the cheapest way of getting them flights was looked into they were offered a look round the city. The old couple preferred just to take it easy, but Goldi and Esther said yes. She wanted to sight-see and maybe shop. Goldi did not mind that, but said more of the harbour as well. A car was arranged and a driver/minder. The man did not seem over-keen, but they were glad to get away from their limited quarters. He drove them up and down many hilly roads. He pointed out the artist areas and some of the older buildings. He stopped once completely. This was to show them a modern road that suddenly ended in mid-air. He told them the city fathers had made a decision that it should not cut through their more picturesque parts.

'I think they are a load of bums. This city needs more decent highways.' He carried on like that a bit more before driving on. Goldi now took the chance to ask him to drop them off at Telegraph Hill. The driver did so, then followed slowly as they stretched their legs. Goldi quite liked looking round, but would not like to have to live there. Next Esther had her hour or so looking round stores. They were driven back to base and had some lunch. Afterwards Esther and Goldi were shown onto a launch that was to take them round much of the harbour. This pleased Goldi no end. There was a two-man crew and one of these acted as their guide. He named the different types of shipping and pointed out various landmarks. When Goldi asked about fishing here he was told on a larger scale it was much like that in Japan. But very few men caught fish

54

as their own food. On land there were vast areas where good oranges grew, but one could only buy orange juice. Here smaller fishing was nearly all for sport. The money paid out for equipment was much more than any value of the fish. Size was what counted for these 'sportsmen'. Goldi thought that was an odd way to carry on. He had known the odd man who enjoyed boasting at home, but they were not well thought of. He began to see that attitudes here mainly revolved around how much cash was available to get the admiration of being top at anything in this country. For himself he preferred to make all he could with his own hands and sail his own boat.

As they moved round this great, natural harbour he could see the layout of the fertile valleys and above the high mountains. He was told that one of these had been a volcano in the past. Goldi thought of the active ones he had left behind in Japan. One of the unusual things back in Hokkaido was the natural hot baths. Even when there was snow on the ground people came from all over the place to use them. Nearby there was a large hotel built in the old style and from there people could walk through covered wooden structures by hot streams. Family groups would often be immersed in the water. Youngsters could play and the old ladies could chat to each other. If the heat got a bit much there was a shallow area like a swimming pool. Most just splashed about. He heard only men actually swam there. Also there was hot mud – a lake of it! Tourists could go up and get a view of that. Some Japanese had even commited suicide by jumping into the depths, mainly women. He had wondered how anybody could be unhappy enough to go to that terrible death. Most Ainu would have more sense, he thought.

Altogether they had five hours with the launch which included a picnic. Esther and Goldi were then returned to their quarters where they told the old couple about their day. This outing had provided a welcome break in a boring routine, but soon they might switch from boredom to fear. Now the time seemed to pass quickly. Soon they would all have to leave San Francisco on the start of the journey to England. All the arrangements had been made between the Jewish group and the immigration people. Poppa Tratski had paid for the tickets and it only remained for them to get to the airport and on board. They were flying from Oaklands and the driver they knew brought a big automobile round. They still did not have much luggage, so just said goodbye and all got into the car. The driver was more communicative this time round.

'I hear none of you have flown before.'

Esther confirmed that.

'Well there is nothing to worry about. I mean the worst would be a crash and that is not likely these days. And on the odd times it does, often quite a lot of people escape. The worst thing is if the fuel goes up. But then it would be too late to worry.'

All these thoughts seemed to put him in a happier state of mind and he said little more. Instead he hummed a tune to himself as they went along. Esther had come across odd bods like him before amongst her own people. She did not translate most of that to the others; best to ignore this Job's comforter. Goldi luckily was more interested in looking out the window to see where they were going. They went along the bridge he had earlier seen from the immigration area and the crossing took some time. Their driver started talking again, almost to himself. 'I had a cousin who crash-landed in a bomber during the war. They were

56

over France when two engines packed up at the same time. That was not usual. And they had a load of bombs still on board. They let that lot go over some fields. I bet that made some farmer swear. The pilot got it down fairly safely, but then they were captured by the Germans.' Now he broke off to whistle instead of humming. 'Of course in those days they were all propeller-driven aircraft. You can't do much gliding with a jet.'

Soon they arrived at the airport and were met by one of Mr Levi's aides. Their driver left with a cheerful wave.

Mr Rheinblatt was rather a quiet man, but he helped them into the building and into comfortable seats. He then fixed them up with refreshments.

They had an hour or so to spare and Mr Rheinblatt encouraged them to watch what went on outside the windows. They could all see the many plane movements which seemed to go smoothly. Goldi was quite surprised how many people strolled around looking relaxed. They looked more like they were going to just buy cigarettes rather than fly. Subconsciously he accepted that many things which were strange to him were commonplace to others.

He found it pleasant to watch the movement of the planes. He also liked to see the passing women. The very young with their pert behinds, shaggy hair, varied bosoms and sunglasses did not interest him much. One or two of the older ones reminded him a bit of Miss Jenkins. There was the possibility he might meet someone like her again. He knew nothing about English women, but he might soon have the chance to find out.

Their protector had been listening to the messages that came over the loudspeakers. He now said, 'Good news. Your plane is now safely down on the tarmac. I will soon see you all onboard.'

With butterflies in their stomachs and small luggages in their hands they followed him out to a waiting bus. Goldi thought, 'We are going by bus? Not plane?' Anyhow they found it drove some distance then they were led up the aircraft steps. At the entrance they all felt worried, but a nice girl made a big fuss of them then said, 'Hurry along now please. We will soon be on our way.'

With further words of encouragement from Mr Rheinblatt they were settled together in the best spot. Esther was by her mother and Goldi by Mr Tratski. The old man was saying something which the girl translated.

'He says should anything happen he wants you to know he regards you almost like a son.' She did not look quite so happy. Before Goldi could say anything the normally silent old lady spoke.

'All this we have to go through, because they say I have a shadow on my lung. Over sixty years I have worked and lived and never been really ill. Why could not a big country find a little corner of America where we could have spent our last days?'

Esther said nothing, because she did not know the answer herself. Also she knew the old lady was also speaking to relieve her nerves. Instead of giving an answer she just held her mother's hand firmly.

'Fasten your seatbelts please,' a voice said. The first young woman had already done those of our party. Mr Rheinblatt told the senior steward they were all innocents as regards flying.

Goldi was flattered by the attention the girl gave them. He was resolved not to show fear in front of her if he could possibly avoid it. Now these girls opened small cupboards in the ceiling and showed the passengers the oxygen masks. This was the usual compulsory drill, but it worried Goldi and his friends who started loud whispering questions. When the girls pointed out the emergency exits they subsided into trembling, silent prayer. I think many ordinary people have a bit of that feeling. It is strange when they really know that now flying causes far less serious accidents that travelling on the roads. With the ramps removed and the engines building up power they knew this was it! When the plane had gained height and levelled out their hearts could go back to their normal places.

'You may undo your safety belts and smoke if you wish,' one girl said. Esther translated for the others. Drinks and snacks appeared and a man dressed as an officer came from the very front and said a few words. Goldi wished he had stayed up there to make sure the plane was safe. Who was on the tiller, or whatever they called it? Nearly everybody else had acted as if all the routine was just that and he saw a few were already asleep! How they could do that when they were higher up than any bird? He thought he deserved a good drink for being quiet during the worst part of the ordeal. It had helped that these rather painted girls were so friendly to all the people they had never met before. Were they a type of flying geisha? After a couple of glasses of vodka he started to get a bit more imaginative. It might be they would get together and do a little dance with singing, but they did not.

Before long he could smell hot food. When that arrived it was so wrapped up it took ages to sort everything out. If they had had a big pot up the front they could have dished out normally he thought. He did the best he could however, leaving all the sweet bits. They did not suit his taste. One of the girls helped

59

the old couple, so they finished with most other people. When everything had been tidied away there was a short lull. Suddenly a lightbeam shot out while the other lights dimmed. Goldi stood up and shouted.

One of the girls came up and said, 'It is all right, nothing to worry about. It is only a filmshow.'

Confused, he sat down again. Esther told him it was not unusual. They often had filmshows in Russia telling of the army or other things their leaders wanted to get across. After some while Goldi's mind sorted out the images he saw projected onto the screen near the pilot's door. There were men and women up there wearing white gowns. He supposed the other passengers were used to this mystery. Looking behind him he saw that a man was fast asleep. Goldi's mind was buzzing so much he thought that a good example and shut his eyes. He did not really sleep, but let his mind go back from his present position. He thought back to when he set sail from the village. Would he even have started if he had known what lay ahead? These speculations did tire him and then he did doze off. When he next opened his eyes the images had gone from the screen. One of the helpful young women stood by his side. 'Do you want to move and maybe look out the window?'

Goldi was not at all keen, but did not want to lose face.

'Is there much to see?'

'Not a lot, you missed the Rocky Mountains which are the most impressive. It's rather flat now.'

'Then no thank you, I will not bother.'

'Where do you come from? I do not recognise your accent.'

He found he did not mind telling her that. He said how he had left home after seeing to the burial of his grandmother. Also about colliding with the other group's boat.

'Well I think you are very brave to travel all this way to a strange country. What do you aim to do in England?'

As Goldi really could not answer that he said, 'I will leave that to the gods' will.'

The girl smiled, then said, 'We will be eating again soon, before we arrive in New York.'

Goldi smiled to himself. What do they give you if you are nervous? You have a chance to drink. If you are all getting bored they feed you. People who fly a lot must have to be careful. With all that and no exercise they must put on too much weight. He thought quite a few of his fellow passengers flew a lot.

Esther had not much time to get bored. She had been too occupied with her parents. They had been very good in a way; just like brave Christians before they were thrown to the lions! On their side they thought a good deal of their daughter and seeing how calm she appeared they did their best to be likewise. Also, once well on their way they saw most of the other passengers looked relaxed. Some of that calm spread to them.

The old couple wondered why they had been so fearful. There were three young children nearby, two boys and a girl. These young Americans had been so involved in some game it was as if they were at home. Momma Tratski thought it would be nice to have some grandchildren like them. Would Esther meet any nice Jewish boys when they reached England? She thought if she lived to be a grandmother she could then die happy.

Poppa Tratski was thinking more of the immediate future. Would he be able to carry on some business in this strange England they were heading for? It was true they were taking quite a good sum of money, but in this new country he would know nobody. As he could not even speak English how could he sell to anyone? He could only pray that the Jewish organisation there was of real help to him. Meanwhile he admired the young women in uniform who did their best to cheer up people like him. He had seen plenty of women working hard in Russia, but they were seldom attractive and did not wear such smart clothes.

At first Esther had to work very hard to look really calm, but she was now quite relaxed. Her thoughts of the future were more exciting than a problem. She had gained a lot of confidence as they all moved forward. She hoped to have even wider horizons once her parents were happily settled somewhere. She was not sure where that would be, but thought life was definitely improving.

They had all eaten enough, even if it was not exciting, and then the announcement came: 'We are now approaching Kennedy Airport. Will all passengers do up their safety belts and extinguish cigarettes?'

Landing is a bit of a test for most people with any imagination. For our group it was much worse. With lights dimming and engine noises different Momma Tratski clutched Esther's arm. She too felt the strain, but acted calm again. Soon the worst was over and they were taxiing towards the terminal buildings. After all this flying they were still in the USA! It was a big, wide country even if not as big-hearted as they might have wished. Our group were told to wait until last when the steps were against the doors. Then the senior steward-ess wished them a good time in New York. They were helped down and then along to a lounge. There a girl in different clothes settled them before a call went out for the Jewish representative. He turned out to be a breezy little man in two-tone shoes.

He greeted them cheerfully and told them what time their plane would be for the UK. He gave Esther a large envelope containing the various papers they would need when they arrived, then introduced them to another young woman. He said she would ensure they got on their plane. After that he said, 'Any questions?' Then he would be off. He shook hands all round, then was away. Well, they thought, things certainly move quickly in New York.

Esther made sure the old couple had all they wanted, then she and Goldi decided to stretch their legs. There were nearly three hours until their plane took off and it was getting dark. They found their way to the top floor of the building where they had a view of some of the taller New York buildings. After looking at those and movements on the ground they went down and looked at the shops. They could not buy much, but it helped to pass the time. They bought some cookies, oranges and grapes before rejoining the old couple. They had been given vouchers for a warm snack and with the bits they bought enjoyed their free time more. They were almost regular fliers now compared to not so long ago.

When their flight was announced the girl returned and stayed until they went on board. Things went much the same, but they did not have a bus ride this time. It was properly dark when they took off and they were able to see New York at its best, ablaze with lights.

They had been nervous on take-off, but nothing like the first time. Another film was shown and this time they saw men in big hats robbing a bank and making off with the cash. It was so exciting Goldi slept for nearly an hour. That was not surprising, as they had been on the move for many hours and were worn out. That made time pass quicker, then it was a breakfast before they were getting ready to land at London Heathrow. The pilot got the plane down smoothly, then they were ready to disembark.

This London certainly looked a bare, modern place. As they had not known what to expect they were not really surprised. A tall girl in uniform spotted them coming down the steps and took them in hand. She got them onto a bus which would take them to Victoria. Esther asked, 'But isn't this London?' The girl smiled and said, 'No, we're in Middlesex.' London proper was about fifteen miles away. At the other end by the coach station a driver would be looking out for the party. His job was to take them to Hampstead where the Society had their HQ. She showed Esther roughly the way they would go and other details. Nothing could go wrong – could it?

The helpful girl settled them into their seats, then they were off. It was not a very interesting journey. After a while somebody said they were on the Great West Road. Goldi did not think it was all that impressive. There were some things he recognised as factories on both sides. These varied in style and names. Firestone was one that seemed to sound familiar, but most others were not. After a while there were not very special houses with slate roofing. Then he just dozed off. Two children there were also bored. They looked at our travellers and asked their parents where these odd people came from. They were shushed into silence for a while afterwards. Goldi had drunk quite a lot before they started. He woke now and felt he needed to get rid of some water. Nobody else seemed to be uncomfortable, but he needed to get out. He reached across and pulled on a handle. The driver then pulled over to the kerb and stopped. Esther had started like all the others. 'What did you do that for?' she asked. When Goldi explained she put her hands to her head. She then had to explain that to the driver. He did not look too pleased, but when they came by some large conveniences he said, 'Now we are here, does anyone else want to go along with this gent?'

Most people shook their heads, but the two children called out *yes!* This meant that Goldi got off with them and their mother. Luckily that trip went off without any more problems. When they all got back on some people took more notice of our group. Goldi of course got most looks, but he was indifferent to that sort of thing. Esther was less than pleased. She wanted to become a smooth town-type. That would not be possible if Goldi carried on his way. When they came to a place called Hammersmith it was time for our group to get off. The driver got off and made a phone call, then said he would wait a few moments to see their pickup come. Soon a large car drew up. Their driver waved and drove on a bit happier.

The new man said very little, but he took their luggage, put it in the boot, settled them all and drove off. It was then a matter of 'Hampstead here we come.'

Chapter Six

When the Tratskis reached the Society's HQ they felt almost as though they had come home. The secretary was there to greet them, then they were handed over to a Russian-speaking colleague. Miss Rostov had got out of Russia fifteen years earlier. Since then she had worked full-time for the Society. She showed them where they could wash, then escorted them to lunch. All their favourite types of food were there, plus kosher butter which was rare in Russia. She chatted to them and made them feel at home. Goldi was a bit on one side, but the atmosphere was friendly and food and drink were things he always enjoyed.

Miss Rostov was then saying they had been found accomodation in a Jewish house nearby and could stay there until more permanent plans were worked out. The only thing she could not be sure of concerned Goldi, as he did not seem to be Jewish. They could help him in the short term and she was just looking to the future. Mr Tratski would be introduced to others who might be able to get him back into some type of business. There happened to be a social gathering planned for a few days' time which might be helpful.

Goldi understood almost nothing this woman said, but Esther translated the points that affected him. For him he asked Miss Rostov if they were near a good river or the sea. That amazed her. 'Why should he want to know that?' she said.

Esther explained he had lived mainly by fishing and enjoyed that way of life. With a bit of humour that was seldom shown she said, 'Maybe he could catch the monster that was said to lurk in the nearby Highgate Ponds.'

When that was translated Goldi wanted to set off then. However Miss Rostov said he would have to wait until the next day when one of the staff could take him there as he exercised his large dog. After all this the car was brought round and she went with them to their new lodgings. They were introduced to the friendly Jewish woman who ran it, then she left them, promising to come back the next day. By the time they had settled in a bit and had a last snack they were ready for bed and all slept soundly.

Goldi was up early the next morning and impatient to meet his new companion. The man had brought a map of the Heath and marked where they would enter it. Goldi had a bundle under his arm. This rather puzzled his companion, but he did not ask about it. They did not have to walk far before the buildings ended and they saw the Heath beginning. Goldi said 'The ponds' a couple of times, because he was anxious to begin the hunt. The man showed him on the map saying it was quite a walk. This did not bother Goldi who felt he needed some good exercise after all that flying. It was still early when they got near the Ponds. The dog was enjoying new smells and the man kept roughly nearby. The only signs of life seemed to be people with their various dogs and one or two horse-riders. Goldi skirted a pond, keeping a sharp lookout. This did not really look like monster water, but he did not want to go back empty-handed, if he could help it.

The day was getting too advanced to think of fishing. There was other prey around he saw. Well-fed ducks. He moved round near some bushes to get nearer to a couple of male mallards. He unwrapped his bundle and took out his bow and an arrow. Near the flight of this he had tied some fine gut. He took careful aim, let fly and was pleased to see it sink into the lower part of a bird's neck. He now pulled in the twine and the bird. 'This will make a nice supper,' he thought.

Just as he twisted the bird's neck and reclaimed the arrow he felt a sharp pain in his ankle. Looking down he saw a small, white dog which was just preparing to give him another bite. He was just about to draw his foot back to give it a kick when he was struck violently on the back of the head once, twice and then a third time.

'I saw you, you savage brute. Not content with killing that poor, defenceless duck you now want to start attacking my dog!'

Goldi saw the speaker was a tall woman dressed in a rough tweed skirt and jacket. In her hand she still clutched the stout walking-stick she had struck him with. For a moment he thought of trying to explain about his hunt for the monster. However he realised that even if she was not so angry he would not find the right words. The woman did not look as though she would stop being very angry he thought. Like a good sailor he now ran before the storm not knowing where his companion was. As he ran she called out, 'I will call the police. We don't want violent killers round our ponds.'

After a while Goldi slowed down. Where was he now? With all that fuss he had lost all sense of direction. Some cloud obscured the sun. He did not know which way to head. He came to a road and headed what he thought was south. Maybe this would lead him to an area he recognised. As he walked a police car drew up alongside him. The driver said, 'Excuse me sir, what are you doing with that duck?' Goldi knew what he was going to do with it, eat it, but he said nothing now. The policeman thought his attitude suspicious. Getting out of the car he said, 'Can I have a closer look?' Goldi handed it over.

'Mm, I see it's been shot with something. Did you do that?' When Goldi nodded the policeman looked grave. He put his hand firmly on the parcel, then said 'Do you mind if I look at this?' When he had unwrapped it and saw the bow, arrow and gut his face hardened. 'I suppose you know that it is an offence to carry a weapon like this around in a public place?'

This got Goldi even more confused. What else was a hunter meant to do than carry his weapons around with him? 'Can I have your name and address sir?' the policeman, getting out his notebook.

'Goldi of Omu,' was the reply.

'And where is Omu exactly.'

'In North Japan.'

The policeman decided he'd had enough. He called up his station to say he was bringing somebody in for questioning.

The desk sergeant looked up in an interested manner when they got into the building. He said, 'Ah, we have just had a lady phone in about a duck being shot and a dog attacked. Now I see you have a very dead duck there. Wait a minute, I think Inspector Large might want to look into this.'

Goldi now began a worrying session of question and answer in a small, rather bare room. After quite a while he managed to explain about the Jewish Society which they seemed to know about. They were put through to the secretary and he soon arrived and was shown into the room.

The inspector said, 'Now sir no charges have been preferred against Mr Goldi yet, although carrying a weapon without licence and disturbing the peace could be appropriate. What we would ask you to do is to ensure he does not roam around London unaccompanied. If there are any similar incidents they will not be overlooked.'

The secretary was far from pleased by this lecture, but he did not want to get on the wrong side of the authorities. He did not manage a smile, but replied, 'Yes, inspector. I am sure that can be arranged between the Society and his friends.'

After some more talk the secretary and Goldi went out to the waiting car. Goldi was feeling rather ashamed of himself. He also was not looking forward to Esther's likely reactions. Very little was said on their journey back.

Surprisingly enough Esther said very little as well. After she had heard all of his adventures she smiled. Instead she spoke about the duck which he had been allowed to bring well-wrapped up.

'You had better get that into the kitchen and cooked while it is still fairly fresh.'

Goldi looked down at the package. It seemed that if you wanted a quiet life in a big city all food had to be bought. Cats, dogs and humans could be fed on the flesh of any animal or fish, but they had to come wrapped, frozen or tinned. Some of these English people seemed to be more concerned about certain animals or birds than people. In his country dogs and cats worked for their living. That did not mean they were never loved however.

71

Goldi took the duck to the landlady to cook for them. She seemed to make rather a fuss about this. He wondered if she wanted it plucked and drawn first. After going back to Esther he found that was not the main problem. Because of their religion they were only meant to eat animals that had been killed in a ritual way. One special type of person had the job of slitting the throat of the bird or animal, so that it bled to death. Goldi knew of that being done to pigs, but he had little real knowledge of English or even Jewish ways. In the end it was agreed the woman would cook it just for him. He ate it later on while the rest had their own type of food. He enjoyed it, but decided he would not eat any of his own kill until things were much different, maybe somewhere else.

The next day Goldi and Esther walked round to the Society HQ to see if there was any news regarding their future in this country. They spoke to Miss Rostov who asked Goldi about the Monster of Highgate Ponds. Somewhat reluctantly Goldi told her what had happened. She did not laugh, but made an odd choking sound a couple of times.

When he had finished she said, 'Well by your description of that lady you may have met up with the Monster after all.'

Miss Rostov was then able to tell them some good news. Enquiries were being made in the Manchester area which could lead to something suitable for the Tratskis' future. For the present through the secretary's effort they were all invited to a small party or social evening. That was tomorrow. Esther wondered if her parents would feel awkward amongst strangers. Goldi asked if any English women would be there, a bit nervously. That made Miss Rostov laugh. 'You need not worry, there will be no English Amazons with sticks,

72

dogs or umbrellas. There should however be an American lady of roughly your age who is a friendly sort, Miss Greenberg.' That had been arranged by the secretary. He had a slight hope it might solve two problems, one of which was Goldi and his awkward ways. Miss Rostov said Esther need not worry about the other people attending. They would either be members, or influential people who supported the work done here. These were likely to go out of their way to be pleasant, as the Tratski family represented a good example for all their set-up here.

Samantha had gone back to using her single name, or maiden name, Greenberg, quite deliberately. She was more than just a casual visitor to the Society. Her father Abe had been born in the state of New York almost sixty-five years earlier. He had grown up in a very liberal Jewish household and felt more American than Jewish. By the time he married at thirty he had made his mark in food sold wholesale. By forty he was a millionaire. He loved his wife Ruby and their daughter, but most of his time had to be taken up with his large business. At the age of fifty-five however he was brought to a sudden halt. One evening his wife said, 'Abe I have a headache, will you get me an aspirin?' After she had taken that he went off into the other room. Then she called out, 'Abe, it's getting much worse!' By the time he reached her she was dead from a cerebral haemorrhage.

At the funeral and long after he pondered his life so far. What were his achievements and what were they worth? He decided not much. He did not make any big announcement, but slowly passed the running of his business over to others he could trust. He tried to give their daughter much more attention and also more to the religion he had been born into. After a painful period of adjustment he became interested in the work of the Society. He put money and effort into it. Although he still had an apartment in New York, he had also acquired a service flat in Golders Green, where he was now staying with his daughter Samantha (Sam). She had grown up with no particular aim and married Toni when aged twenty-three. He was a young executive she had met while working in an advertising agency. It had seemed a good marriage to her, but suddenly she was heading for a divorce. It turned out he had met another girl through his family who meant more to him than Sam. As the marriage had not taken place in a church or synagogue his family did not regard it as very binding. His second marriage not all that long after took place in a Catholic church with full ceremony. What with that and then the sudden death of her mother Sam had suffered a breakdown in mind and body for a while. More recently she had started to feel a lot better and was now a partner in her father's new interest.

The Tratskis and Goldi felt nervous when they got to the familiar Society's HQ. The party had started and they were soon put at ease. They were introduced to all the guests including the Greenbergs. Goldi was quite taken with Sam's appearance. She had dark brown hair of medium length, wore little make-up and was of average height. Also she did not have the penetrating voice which is quite common among some American women. There was a slight trace of hair upon her upper lip, but nothing to compare with that of long-remembered Miss Jenkins.

When they had all eaten and taken a glass of wine or juice the guests spread themselves in the downstairs rooms. Mr Greenberg asked the Tratskis if they could join them in their quiet corner.

'I hear you have had a few adventures already,' he said to Goldi, who wondered if this referred to the Ponds incident. Mr Greenberg continued, 'I suppose it is just as hard for you to get used to a big town as it would be for me to live by fishing.' It took a while for this to get across, but Esther was able to do that. Goldi just shrugged and smiled. It seemed to be the safest thing to do.

'I tell you what. Why don't we all have a day looking around London? I have been quite busy and it would give me pleasure also.'

After quite a bit of discussion it was decided that Goldi, Esther, Sam and Mr Greenberg would go, as the old couple of townies were not keen on that experience. Mr G. might be able to take them somewhere quieter, but interesting later on. It was agreed the next day would be as good as any for the younger ones.

At 10.00 a.m. the Greenbergs arrived at the door in an expensive-looking limousine complete with driver.

'I normally drive myself,' said Mr Greenberg, 'but in central London it is almost impossible to park and this will give us more freedom to walk about.' He had not wasted his time in London and knew more about it than most lifelong residents. He got the driver to go past St Pancras Station where they saw the stylish hotel which is one of Sir Gilbert Scott's most impressive creations. They got out for a while at Gray's Inn Gardens to enjoy that stretch of well-kept greenery. Even with the traffic passing nearby this is very restful compared to all the bustling town life that surrounds it. They drove over Blackfriars Bridge to Southwark. He told them how for a long time only old London Bridge and ferrymen connected the major parts of London on the north bank to the south. They walked along a scruffy little street where he was able to point out the house with its plaque that had housed Sir Christopher Wren. Each day that gentleman had been rowed across the Thames to supervise his work in building the new St Paul's Cathedral. The sight and smell of this rather brown river roused Goldi's interest and he asked many questions. Abe answered those he could. He explained how the river used to be much wider and shallower. Nevertheless as the roads were so bad it was for a long time the main highway of London. The rich and powerful had expensive boats with uniformed men to look after them. The Royal Barge would often have been seen going to and from Hampton Court.

From the south side they saw the Palace of Westminster. By Lambeth Palace they got out to look into the grounds. This building was in the old style and had up to fairly recent times produced a good quantity of food from its large, walled gardens. It had likely done so in World War II when even strips of grass by main roads had grown vegetables. Goldi would have liked to keep following this river, but Abe said that would swallow up all the time. However, after a snack they went through Horse Guards Parade into St James's Park. There Goldi was pleased to see more water sparkling. Abe led the way with Esther, while Goldi followed with Sam. He showed signs of getting excited when he saw all the water-fowl and pigeons so close, but a warning touch on his arm reminded him these had to be treated like pets in this odd town of London.

Abe told them at certain times the keepers fed the pelicans whole fish. They did not see that however. Abe gave Esther some stale bread he had brought and she enjoyed feeding all these different birds that came so close. They drove round Trafalgar Square, then slowly past Buckingham Palace. They walked along the edge of Hyde Park, but not where Goldi might see the rowing-boats. He had no wish to be taken on the water. Abe did not want fishing lessons either. He took them by Speakers' Corner and tried to describe the British idea of democracy: say what you like, but mainly do what you are told.

Esther was getting into this sight-seeing idea. At Marble Arch they walked up to it along the subway, passing music-making buskers. There were both fellows and girls. Some played classical violin music, there were all sorts. The Arch had once been by Buckingham Palace, but was moved here onto the site of the Tyburn Tree. Now Goldi's ears pricked up. He asked if this tree had borne any special fruit. Abe with an odd smile had said yes in a way. He described how years back men and women had been publicly hanged here for crimes ranging from murder down to being a well-known purse-snatcher. That surprised Esther a bit. From what she had seen of the English, most seemed a lot softer or kinder than the Russians. She had heard back there even under the czars quite a few people who had committed murder were not executed. If the state was not involved the person could often be sent off to Siberia or some similar bleak place. Abe was not going into that, but knew that where Russia was vast the UK was very small.

Esther and Sam would have liked to see some shops, but Abe said they could do that another time without any men. Off Oxford Street they looked round St Giles Parish Church. There back in those 'good old days' convicted criminals on their way to the Tree used to be given a cup of strong wine. That would have made the rest of that trip slightly less awful. Not all that far away Goldi looked up at the Centrepoint and asked if that was the tallest building then in London. He was

77

told no, and then they were driven to see the Post Office Tower. 'That may not be the highest, as they keep putting up new office buildings, but none as high as ours in New York,' Abe said. Not far away they were able to go into a Jewish salt-beef place. There they all enjoyed a good meal. The younger ones could have gone on even more, but Abe had done his job well enough he thought and looked forward to putting his feet up.

'It's all right for you young ones, but you've got to remember I'm an old man now,' Abe said. He was pleased when the women said he still seemed young to them. It was agreed Sam could take on any other outing if needed. They would still have use of the car and driver. Abe told them he was going back to the States for some business he needed to do.

Esther thanked them both on behalf of herself, her family and Goldi. The women got on well enough to enjoy a good shop. Really Esther could not afford more than a few items, but window-shopping is a big deal for many people.

The next day was typically English with low clouds and lots of rain, but the Tratskis had plenty to occupy their minds. The Society had got everything arranged for them in Manchester. They were to travel up there in four days' time. They would have use of a good-sized flat with plenty of furniture supplied. It was over a Jewish clothiers place. Mr Tratski and the two women would be able to work from there for three months to see how things worked out. This was good news, especially for the old couple who were not used to just sitting around all day. They had been very grateful for all the help they had received so far in this small country, but enforced leisure was not for them while they had some energy left. Secretly Esther was not sure she wanted to stay in the same line as them. She hoped Manchester would prove to be big enough to give her more scope later on. For the time being she would of course try to get her parents on their way again.

The snag Esther saw most involved Goldi. There would be space enough for him to stay with them, but what would keep him safely occupied? She did not want him out on the loose with them all occupied getting settled. She would find out that Manchester had new offices, factories and shops. It also had some older buildings left intact after the war including attractive warehouses. There were mills, libraries, two rivers and a canal that took biggish boats. But it did not seem the right sort of place for someone with Goldi's interests. The secretary was pleased when Abe made a suggestion over this problem. He said, 'While I'm in the States Sam and Goldi can stay in our apartment. There is room enough.' He hoped Sam would like this suggestion. He was a pretty good judge of character. He knew Goldi was not a complex character, even if he was restless. He did not have the veneer of civilisation which most people try to hide behind. Despite his size and bold appearance Abe was sure that Sam would have no bother in keeping him in check. He also knew that she would really rather care for a person than a cause. He might be too old to seek a new companion, but he would be content to see his only daughter a bit happier. This child-man might possibly fit the role.

The weather next day, although changeable, was much better. Sam, Esther and Goldi thought they had better have their outing while they had the chance. They did not make use of the car. Instead they went by bus, Underground, taxi or walked. Abe had insisted Esther take £25. He was also helping Goldi and said would she buy a keepsake for him and herself? She did not like taking money, but knew he would be upset if she refused. She was fond of him and he had promised to visit the Tratskis when they had settled down more Manchester way. It certainly felt nice to have some money to spend.

They got the Northern Line down to Leicester Square with no trouble. Esther was still nervous and so was Goldi, but Sam's presence made them less so. His footwear was now in a sorry state. It had been made for boats and grasslands, not London pavements. He would not even try normal styles, but was happier when a few moccasins were dug out from somewhere by the tired assistant. Having got a pair they carried on. Esther liked it round Regent Street, but Goldi found it too noisy and busy. However they did get him into a couple of large stores near Oxford Circus. Quite a few English husbands would have given him some pity with that. Afterwards they went into Berwick Market which was quite crowded, but more to his taste. There was plenty of good fruit and veg on the stalls and more interesting items. Down Brewer Street he saw a very well-stocked fish shop. He pointed out a box of frozen octopus and was delighted to see the live eels. They nearly had to pull him away from there.

They had had to go by quite a few strip clubs. These with their pictures of half-naked buxom girls did not interest him at all. He did like the lights and jangling from the amusement arcades. The many gambling machines he passed, but liked trying to catch a watch or other gift with the shiny cranes. Not winning after several goes they went by Gerrard Street where they were all surprised to see the large number of Chinese people there. Goldi wondered what they were doing there. He thought these English people were quite mixed up for some reason.

After a light meal and a rest Sam suggested they get off the noisy streets and look at Regent's Park. There they walked round the lake and Queen Mary's Gardens. She considered the zoo, but decided against that not knowing what Goldi might get up to there. Instead she told them about the open-air theatre that was open on summer evenings, then they made their way back home.

Chapter Seven

The day soon came when the Tratskis had to leave for Manchester. Miss Rostov would see them into their railway compartment and it was arranged that they would be met at the other end. It was thought best that they say their goodbyes at the Society's HQ before they got into the car that was taking them to Euston. Esther took this occasion calmly enough, but the older couple made more of a fuss which surprised nobody. Poppa Tratski kissed Goldi on both cheeks and hugged him. Mrs Tratski gave him a peck on the cheek, then started quietly crying into a handkerchief. Goldi did not show a lot, but he also was moved after all they had shared together. He said he wanted to hear how things went with them all. Mr Greenberg promised that and said he and Sam would go up to Manchester before too long as well. 'I've heard it's less than three hours by Intercity and what's that? No time at all,' Abe said.

Esther stood back a little from all this. She was more pleased than otherwise to be going and looked very nice in the dress she had bought on that shopping expedition.

'You know,' said Abe, looking at Mr Tratski, but speaking so they all could hear, 'If I was twenty years younger I'd be tempted to come courting your daughter.'

Goldi said, 'I too would like to come and see you all in that place called Manchester.'

Sam said, 'Well I daresay that could be arranged without too much trouble later on.'

After more exchanges and hugs the Tratskis then left for their new lives.

A day or so earlier they had all attended a service at the local synagogue. Abe had suggested this in one of his more serious moods. The others including Goldi all agreed. He did not know what was involved, but understood the idea of a ceremony before a big event. Abe's big car had soon taken them the couple of miles involved. They were dropped off outside a newish-looking building. It was decorated over the large door-way with an ornate candelabra in a type of shiny stone. Goldi thought that looked very good. Esther had told him to bring his smarter hat. That had surprised him, as it was nice weather still. He decided the fur one would be too hot, so brought his cleaned skin cap.

When Abe came along Goldi was surprised to see he was wearing a black coat with a large, black hat like Mr Tratski. Abe normally wore light-coloured clothes and went bare-headed. The women were also dressed in dark, modest clothes. As they all went into the building Goldi went to take off his hat, as he had learnt to do in England, but Esther shook her head. He wondered if he should take off his shoes, but copied the others and left them on. That was different to the way in Japan. Once they got inside he saw a number of men with good beards, so did not feel odd about his. One man who was obviously a priest led the service. He sang and also chanted much of it. Goldi did not try to follow the words, but he was enjoying the unusual experience and the feeling of fellowship. Many of the English he had seen around the town seemed to do their best never to speak or even look at another man. When he was not sure how to act he just copied Mr Tratski. Although he knew he looked a stranger he made no big mistakes and felt quite pleased with himself.

After they came out of the synagogue Sam said she would like to walk back for the exercise. Goldi felt that would be good and joined her. As they walked she asked him about the Ainu religion. Talking to somebody he knew he did not do too bad. He said that although the Japanese sometimes tried to ignore them they did have very different ways in worship. Much of his talk was of the various ways they regarded and treated bears when they were well away from town people like he had been. She did not make any comment on that when he finished and they walked for a while in silence. She then asked about his former wife and children. He told her, going right back to his childhood in the village. Again she made no comment. Quite soon it seemed they reached the Society's HQ, so it was a very one-sided conversation.

Goldi quite soon adjusted to living with the Greenbergs. It was good also to have comfortable rooms just for himself. Solitude at sea or in the open country was often quite enjoyable, but he did not fancy it in London. When Abe flew off to the States he was quite happy with the situation he left behind. He thought Sam seemed to be benefiting from it already.

Apart from Goldi and the Tratskis Sam had other things she was involved with in the Society and they took up much of her time. She could not take Goldi with her generally, but they got out into the open air regularly. Sometimes on a nice evening they had a meal served outside a pub or café. One Sunday afternoon they went back to Hyde Park where they listened to a military band for nearly an hour. Goldi was mainly impressed by their colourful dress uniforms. He thought they all must be very important men to wear such clothes with silver tassels over the bright colours. Sam tried to explain some things like that to him, but was not sure he understood. He had thought England must be very rich to be able to employ men so smart to entertain people like them. By Whitehall others in shiny hats and piped leather trousers just sat on their horses all day. If this couple had seen the same men wearing overalls working on armoured cars or training on Salisbury Plain they would have been amazed. Sam said England had a very rich heritage, so maybe that is where the money came from.

A bit later that made Goldi quite thoughtful. He guessed that Sam and her father would not worry about that, but he did not want just to be kept by them at his age and still healthy. If he could not get a living by fishing there had to be other ways.

Now they walked past lovely flowerbeds and saw a wide road made of sand (Rotten Row). Here people in smart clothes of a different type rode well turned-out horses. That was another sign of wealth, he thought. In his country if anybody could have got a horse it would have been used for ploughing, taking loads up from the beach or something of that sort. Sam said these people just did this for a bit of pleasure. Goldi asked if they could learn, but Sam did not seem to be keen on that sort of thing.

'Let's just walk on a bit and see what else there is to do,' Sam said with a little smile to herself. In a few minutes Goldi saw a stretch of water ahead, yes, and people in boats! What had they they found here? The truth was they had found the damned-up Westbourne or stream. King George II had ordered this to be done when he owned the area as ruler. By his decision we now have the Serpentine instead of the previous number of small ponds. As times changed this then became something for the people to enjoy instead of just the King and his friends.

Goldi's eyes gleamed with pleasure. It seemed ages since he had heard water lapping under the keel of a small boat. He tried to hurry Sam forward, but with a grin she said, 'No hurry big boy. Nobody is going to pull the plug out.'

'Can we go out in a boat or do those people own them?' he asked. He did not think they were boat-owners, because many could hardly control their craft and he saw some near-collisions.

'Yes we can go out for an hour or so if you like. All the boats are for hire.'

Goldi saw a little hut on a platform built out over the lake and urged Sam towards it. She paid for two hours and hoped they'd be back by then. He stood impatiently by as she did this. Then they walked towards a small rowing boat that was just being returned. Sam put her hand firmly on Goldi's arm and said, 'No we can't go on that one, we will have to wait our turn.'

'But we are right here now, what's to stop us?'

Sam pointed to a number of people standing between metal rails who were beginning to stare at them.

'Those people were here before us and we have to queue like them.'

'Well if they had hurried over they could have got to this boat first.'

With difficulty, but firmness, Sam explained how British people had been encouraged to learn this way mainly in the last war. If everybody dashed together there could be injuries or worse. She said it was a little like the Japanese taking off their shoes to enter a house or temple. Goldi knew about that, but still found it all a bit odd. That bit about Japan was true, but otherwise they tended to fight for anything else unless teachers or police kept order. Nevertheless they joined the line. They got some funny looks, but did not bother about that. Then these others got some entertainment by listening to their conversation.

After about thirty minutes they got a boat. Goldi had never handled one like this before, but fairly soon got the hang of it. He saw some who were proficient and copied them also. Sam was not all that much of an outdoor-type, but would rather sit in a boat than try to control a horse. She had tried to learn when she was young, but found those animals had four corners which moved erratically. From this boat she got a good view and noticed how things looked fresh and green for the most part in England. The water did not look too good, but then nor did it in some harbours. They skirted a small, duck-laden island and headed for the bridge. 'Look, fishermen,' Goldi called out. He doubted there was much in there, but he still enjoyed the sight. A few people were looking over the parapet of the bridge. A small boy called out, 'Go it fungus-face,' before being pulled away by his annoyed mother.

Goldi was so enjoying himself that he did not even hear all this, but Sam smiled to herself. She told him when they were getting near the end of the boating section, then they circled round more slowly. There were some hardy swimmers and more sunbathers. She would have chosen somewhere cleaner and warmer, but Sam could share their enjoyment. The ducks were not bothered by the boat and soon got out of their way. These also Goldi hardly noticed. At last he had burnt up his spare energy, so Sam then had a go. They used an oar apiece, but mainly went in circles. After that she was not sorry when their time was up. They walked over the bridge, then had some refreshments in the café. He would have gone back to the boats. Instead Sam led them along until they reached the Albert Memorial. Goldi really liked that and the round pond. There serious men sailed very good model boats in a serious way. A smallish boy had a motor boat, but that had broken down. Goldi would have waded in to retrieve it, but Sam saw the breeze would soon bring it in. Goldi liked the tall ships most, as they were so elegant. After a while he got talking to an elderly owner about the rigging and technical matters. These men looked vastly different, but they shared an enthusiasm. They stayed there until the light was fading, then went home.

Esther meanwhile was adjusting to her new environment. It had been a trouble-free trip up to Manchester where they had met their future employer, a Polish Jew named Golishewski. He had been a prisoner under the Russians, so could speak their language. Later they found he was bitterly anti-Soviet. That attitude did not apply to refugees like themselves however. Before World War II Poles were divided into quite separate classes. When the Russian influence became the main factor there was a big upheaval. Some bent with the storm and survived fairly well, while those who could got out. The others remaining had a very bad time. The Polish ones had separate problems in addition. Mr Golishewski had got to Britain at the end of the war and had stayed ever since. He married an English Jewess and they had two daughters, then with his wife they got a small business going. That had built up very well. He was a short man with a sharp tongue, but a warm heart.

'You can call me Jan, although English people call me John,' he said as he met them off the train. When they first started out they had lived over the shop and he worked eighteen hours a day. Now prosperous and with the the girls almost grown up he was going to take things easier. Also he was just coming up to sixty. He had bought a neat, well-built house in Glossop. They were already set up there. Although it was only twelve miles from Manchester the area was like another world. They still got the rain, but this was part of the Peak District with long views and all the fresh air one could wish for. From the Ship Canal to Derwent Dale was like a mental leap. Most of Mr Golishewski's business was now done through his warehouse which was spacious. However, he wanted to keep on the old shop premises. He would see if this family settled down all right there. If they didn't they could rent the flat and maybe get work elsewhere. His daughters had grown up with real Manchester accents and knew no other. With this old couple he enjoyed using his Russian again. Esther's English was on a par with this. That would be useful in the business he knew. She must have a quick mind which was also an asset.

Jan now led them out of the station and settled them in his big estate car. 'You will find it mild up here, but rather wet,' he said. Judging by the amount of water being thrown off the windscreen, Esther believed him. She thought the area around the shop looked depressing when they stopped. She had not realised it, but she had been spoilt by the stay in London. People who live in the likes of Dagenham. Tooting, Walthamstow or Tottenham see a very differ-

90

ent side of London. The plum parts are Hampstead, Chelsea, Putney or Richmond. The Tratskis had started off very well, but now were being brought down to earth.

'I'll show you upstairs, then leave you with my wife,' Jan said. He knew she had got a meal ready and would settle them in okay. 'I am busy this afternoon, but will see you again about ten tomorrow morning. Then I can show you downstairs and some of the town.'

Mrs Golishewski was a large red-haired woman. Her voice was a bit loud, but she meant no harm. She showed them round the flat with its two bedrooms, kitchen, bathroom and large living-room. It was not showy, but of decent size and comfortably furnished. She found it hard to speak to the old couple, so spoke to Esther.

'If you want to wash your hands dear, then you could help me dish out the meal. I haven't done anything fancy, just stew. Later on I'll show you the local shops where you can get essentials. For anything else you would need to get a special bus into the main part.'

Esther could not argue with all this, so just nodded.

They soon had their meal served and eaten. After that Mrs Golishewski showed the old couple how to use the small electric water heater over the sink. She then left them to wash up while she and Esther went out.

Esther had never been inside an English self-service place before, so she watched and learnt. Next they called into a Greek greengrocers. There they were served and it felt a lot more human. They only came out with a bag of oranges, but Esther had been quite surprised to see a collection of red and green peppers there and other odd items. Before they came out she said to the owner, 'Please what are these called?' The

91

things she pointed out were pale green, about four inches long and came to a point at one end. The man smiled. 'We call them Ladies Fingers. They are very nice cooked with lamb or other things like that.'

Next they walked past first a bakers, then a butchers. Mrs Golishewski said, 'I don't buy there. There is a good kosher shop not much further.' They went in and Esther was introduced to the owner.

'What do they sell in that shop next door?' Esther asked.

'Oh I don't think you would want that, it is a tripe shop.'

That name intrigued Esther and she asked for details, but after she agreed it did not sound very appealing. There was all the bleaching, then the cooking with milk and onions. Mrs G. also told her about black pudding, but that would be against all that they believed. Faggots and other odd items did not really sound attractive either. Esther had eaten octopus in Japan which was okay she remembered. They were now at a bus stop. When the bus came Esther was helped to ask for the right stop and paid the fares. When they got off it was only a short walk to the flat (which was just as well if it was rainy weather Esther thought). When everything had been put away in the right cupboards Mrs Golishewski said her goodbyes, then left to drive home.

The next morning they were shown round the store downstairs, then Jan drove them into the city centre. He also showed them the ship canal, the musical college and some of the fine, old warehouses. Esther found this area much more interesting and they were lucky to get some sunshine. It stayed dry all the time. However she promised to buy herself a good umbrella very soon.

This store only had one man and a boy there. Jan had not built up the staff as he wanted to see how the Tratskis managed. He did not have to worry, as they soon got into it. Mr Tratski found the little English he had picked up went quite a long way in business. Things were not the same as in Russia, but there were many similarities. Momma Tratski could not get on with any strangers, but she could do her part in the background. On the Sabbath they were introduced into the synagogue and made very welcome. Religious observance had been very hard in Russia, but here there were no such problems. After this introduction they made it there at least once a week. It was not just for the religious side, but to meet others from Eastern Europe. Before long they got to know other non-English folk. Jan dealt with exiled Poles and these sometimes came into the shop. One friendly man was named Alfred Kipura. He often stayed on after the business was settled, as long as they were not too busy. Although he was fifty-five he had never got married and was still a bit boyish in his ways. He often liked to talk to Esther who was too soft-hearted to rebuff him. Alfred still had a mother alive in Poland and his father had only died four years ago. Ten years earlier Alfred had been able to go home for a holiday. There he had bought a raffle ticket in his father's name. There was a shock when he won the very large prize. However, because of the law he was not allowed to take any money out of the country, only what he had brought. Because of this he spent it on a very nice house. He proudly showed Esther a photo that he kept in his wallet. It was a very good-sized place standing in its own grounds. He had established his mother downstairs and for now a cousin lived above. In England he just lived in a furnished room in an old part of

Manchester, but obviously felt good to be a man of property. Esther wondered if she also was meant to fall for the place and take Alfred with it. She did not think that would work. She did not want to be a replacement for his mother when that time came.

Mr Tratski sometimes spoke about Goldi, wondering if they should get him nearby. Esther was against that as this was not his sort of place. He needed openness, even rather wild areas, preferably near the sea. At the end of a month Mr Tratski got her to write to Goldi and also sent him some cash. Esther had said that was not necessary, as Sam was looking after all that, however she let him have his way. Mr Tratski said, 'A man needs some money of his own, it's not right to be dependent on a woman.'

Goldi was pleased to get the letter and cash. He would use it somewhere. Sam had been quite busy but one Saturday she said to him, 'I think you would enjoy a trip by boat up to Kew, does that sound a good idea to you?' He said, 'I don't know anything about the place, but a boat trip is always good.' It was well into summer now and for a change it was good weather that year. In Hokkaido there had been very short summers and then it would be sweaty hot, followed by bitter winter weather. This country seemed much more gentle even if not all that reliable regarding the seasons. As Japan was all extremes did that tend to make the people like that too?

They got out sharp the next day and made their way to Westminster. Sam knew the time of the boat, so they only had a short wait. The bustle around and the river flowing by kept Goldi happy enough meanwhile. When the boat tied up at the mooring he saw it was rather old, but not bad. There had been some movement along the river and some bigger craft were permanently moored nearby. If Goldi could have seen it a hundred years earlier he would have seen it full of activity with barges being unloaded by pulleys, men sweating and the area crowded with men. Those days had however long passed. Now a river police boat went by and Sam had to tell him all she could about that. The crew looked at this odd couple as they passed. Once they were underway (with little fuss) one of the crew started explaining bits of history concerning the Tower of London, Traitors Gate etc. This saved Sam from any more work. Apart from Battersea Power Station Goldi was not very interested. It was movement he enjoyed most. When they passed Chelsea Reach he asked about who lived on those little boats. Some people were on the move on these in the nice weather. Sam could not tell him much and didn't want him to get the idea of obtaining one. She thought it a dirty smelly place to live, but kept that to herself.

When Goldi learned that most of these boats were never moved he lost interest. For him a craft was a living thing or nothing, just a hulk. These people might just as well have built a hut on the bank.

They soon passed Fulham Palace, then the football ground. He asked Sam what football was. She explained it was almost a religion in this country. Many men never entered a place of worship, but every week went to these grounds whatever the weather and always in winter. In the US it was the same with baseball. Goldi was not religious, but he saw much more point in that than watching men kicking a ball about. Soon they were being told about the university boat race. Now that was more like it he thought. Sam told him what she could and he thought that was what Englishmen should all be like. They had a much kinder country than Japan with a good coast, but that was thought little of by these strange people. To give a great deal of time and sweat on one short row on this river was much more to be admired.

An elderly couple had been sitting nearby. The man adjusted his trilby hat and said, 'I hope you don't mind me poking my oar in, but I could tell you a lot about this river.' He then said how he had worked for years as a tally clerk on a wharf by the Tower of London and talked about all the coastal shipping they used to handle. His friend had slipped off a barge and fallen in. He seemed okay when they got him out, but a couple of days later this man had died of a broken neck. He also said about all the working men who also took part in river races every year and the rituals they observed. This was not history, but much of it was still kept up, but did not get the publicity of the Oxford and Cambridge events. 'These men are real Londoners, those at the big race are from all over and just share an enthusiasm. Much of the East End was knocked down and Londoners scattered, but the spirit does not die.'

Goldi listened to all this with interest and like his people had respect for the knowledge of the old. Sam was less taken, but they thanked this couple before going below for a drink. After that they went back on deck, refreshed.

By the time they reached Kew it was lunchtime. Most of the pleasure boats that go up have been in service for many years. If the tide is against them it can be a very slow business. Goldi and Sam had been lucky. She said, 'I think we should go over the other side of the river and have something to eat before exploring the gardens.' That suited Goldi who was always ready for his food. They went into a very smart public house where there was a very good buffet. After they walked a little into Brentford which historically was very important. Outside another rougher-looking pub there was a big stall. There Goldi saw they sold cockles, mussels, jellied eels and winkles by the pint. They did not need any of these and Sam was glad to get away from the strong smells that held him. Then they crossed over to the gardens. Here they wandered around doing the usual thing. Goldi was very interested in the pagaoda which gave the Japanese touch. Sam liked the small palace, but that did not interest him. He did like the royal beasts outside the tropical glass-house. Sam could not tell him anything of those, but they went inside. The humidity was to be expected, but they did not need too much of that and soon went back into the open air. Sam had brought some bits of bread and fed these to the ducks who were always on the lookout. 'Come on,' she said to Goldi, 'you give them some as well.' This was very much going against the grain for him but he did so to keep the peace. Sam had done this deliberately, because although she had time to spare she did not always want to have to watch him in case of trouble. He was behaving much better and she was pleased about that and more relaxed. They went into a smaller glasshouse where cucumbers hung down and large fish swam around. They went between the elaborate rockeries with their special plants and little waterfalls. She also showed him the tall brick water tower that was nearer the road. They then bought ice creams and sat quietly eating those for some time. In another house there were plenty of oranges and lemons growing and all was well cared-for. They had another sit down on a shady seat looking across the lake at a smaller building which was the museum and later looked inside. The giant plants nearby reminded her of very prickly rhubarb. Next

97

they wandered for quite a while in the wooded, wilder part of the grounds, then out onto the riverbank. After walking along they were glad to reach another pub. Goldi bought a bottle of vodka and got Sam some chocolates while she visited the ladies. As she still had not come out he topped his beer up with vodka and had a good drink. 'Why are you drinking that?' she said when she did reappear.

'Well, you were such a long time, I got you some chocolates,' he replied. He did not like being told off and went on, 'Well Mr Tratski being Russian I thought it a good idea to spend his money on something Russian.'

After she looked at the bottle Sam said, 'Well this is vodka, but it's made in the good-old USA.' That did not make Goldi any happier and he stayed silent. However, by the time she had finished her drink and they were out on the riverbank again the spirit was taking effect on Goldi. What was that he could see in the river? That was not a common duck, it was a black-necked goose! This brought all his old hunting instincts back. He did not have a spear or bow and arrow, but he would try to catch the bird. Despite Sam's cry he now proceeded to climb down the steep embankment. The bird was in shallow water, so he should be able to catch it quite easily. However, after he left the brick embankment he found he was in thick mud. Normally that would have been enough to stop him, but he'd be sober then. Now he just waded on. Sam called out once more, then went back to the pub and a stiff drink. When she emerged a very messy Goldi was sitting on the footpath and the goose was far away. By now Goldi was not looking at all lively and was vainly trying to get some of the mud off his clothes. Sam did not say much and after quite some while they were driven home in a taxi – Goldi wrapped up in four Sunday newspapers.

After this episode Sam decided she would have to get Goldi right away from London or any other large place. These obviously did not suit him and she could not play 'nursemaid' to him all her life. The first thing was to get him new clothes. These might be able to be cleaned, but she thought he really needed a new life and the clothes to go with it. In London any style except nudity is barely noticed, but ten miles away even, it is a different story. In Buckinghamshire or Dorset you need to merge in, at least a bit. The next day Sam went out and bought T-shirts and jeans of Goldi's size, then they headed for Oxford Street. Most of the shops there cater for women, but there are a few for men. They went in one and the assistant measured Goldi before bringing a selection. He went into a cubicle, but soon looked out wanting help. Sam told the assistant who was only to happy to help 'Big Boy'. That attitude could have started a fight, but Goldi restrained himself.

After they had left the assistant chatted to his friend. 'What do you think that fellow wanted help with?' 'Don't ask me,' the other replied. 'Well he didn't even know how to zip up his flies. I happened to touch him then and he got quite annoyed. As if I'd do that on purpose.' 'No of course not,' said his friend.

Footwear was another problem for Goldi. The moccasins were not too bad, but anything else was no good for him. He told Sam and in the end she had to pay a very high price for the softest leather boots she could find. It was lucky money was no problem in her family. This outing had been enough for both of them and they were glad to get home where he tried the things on again and showed her. Sam had been thinking

99

about Goldi's beard as well. This large growth was okay in the synagogue, but outside was a bit outsize.

'Hey, what say you have your beard trimmed up a bit? You've certainly got enough to look after there.' Goldi could have not been more shocked if she had suggested he take his trousers off for her. Unless he'd been drinking he would not normally argue with her, but this was different.

'No,' he replied. 'The beard is a sign of manhood to us. We do not cut it for anyone.' She let the matter drop then, but still kept it in her mind. After some while she thought of one possibility. Some writers like Tolstoy had been notorious for their oversized whiskers, but ignored any criticism 'All right then,' she said, 'tomorrow we will shop for good outdoor clothes, then look for a tape-recorder you can use to record your various experiences.'

'Why should I want to do that?' Goldi said. She soothed him saying, 'Don't worry your whiskers about that now, just leave all that to Sam.'

Their next outing was to Knightsbridge where she sought writer-type clothes for his large frame. He was getting into all these outings and looked at the Underground map up by the carriage top.

'Aren't we near that park where we went rowing?' he asked. Now she saw some of the disadvantages of teaching the illiterate to read.

'Yes,' she said, 'but we won't have time to go there today. We might have time later to pop into the Natural History Museum. I think you would enjoy looking at their things and with many you can make them come to life.' He did not understand what he meant, but it sounded quite interesting and stopped him carrying on. He would be very glad to get back to something like the life he had led in Hokkaido. If he had Sam as his companion that would be ideal, but the way of life was the most important thing to him.

They came out of the Underground and walked to the store in the rain. Goldi was very impressed when they got in there. Here there was no hustle and bustle, nobody came asking them, did they need help? It was more like a church than a store. After a long while however a quiet-looking man did come up. 'Can I be of assistance?' They told him and were ushered further on. In the end Sam got Goldi a three-quarter length waterproof, windproof coat. This would have looked good on a Canadian lumberjack. Further on he spotted a deerstalker hat.

'I'd like one of those,' Goldi said. Sam was not too sure, but soon he was the proud owner. Well okay now let's see if they have a suit to match it. With plus-fours and a stout stick they looked like author and secretary. They did not get a tape-recorder, but were told of a good place for another time. Despite the weather they then walked on to the Natural History Museum.

When they went into the gallery where a large whale was the main exhibit Goldi was thrilled. In Japan he had seen some of these from a distance when they have been harpooned, but never close-by like this. After quite a while there they went round other parts. He could not understand about the prehistoric exhibits and she soon gave up trying to explain. Why had he never seen them? What planet had they arrived from and when? When she said some had come from just outside London he did not call her a liar, but did not believe her either. She said they would have been trapped and then killed by short men in skins like him, but painted blue. They would only have had wooden weapons or rocks. When they finally left they went into a local pub. It was getting late however, so they only had time for a quick drink. They started walking towards Gloucester Road Station, then saw a rather scruffy Fish & Chip place. Sam would normally have avoided this, but with the cold and damp they rushed inside and sat down. Nobody came forward for quite a while, but a smiling man appeared as their voices got louder. He asked what they would like and got a very big order. As the food was being cooked his wife brought them big mugs of tea and bread and butter which they soon reduced to crumbs.

Goldi had not given Sam any problems regarding sex. He was just a problem when not being watched properly. Since her unhappy marriage she did not want to know. He had left two children back in Japan of course. He regarded her as a bit of a mother figure. That was okay, but not at all flattering to her. She found it best just to deal with the problems as they came along – it was at least better than boredom. Now she wondered where to start regarding getting Goldi located somewhere suitable. The Tourist Board might have some knowledge of areas with free fishing and the like. He could cook anything he caught using old, traditional ways she knew. Although quiet she also wanted somewhere that could be reached without too much trouble from London, so all this was not going to be easy. She wanted to get it all sorted before the end of the year if possible. She sent a cable to her father explaining all this and got the go-ahead back. She now started with all the contacts she had in the country to make things happen quickly and soon got some leads. Quite a few of these were no good, but she tried them. She also had an invite from some good English friends to spend a weekend with them, and accepted, taking Goldi as well.

Bruce and Wendy were nice people with knowledge

and experience. They were soon made comfortable without any questions starting. After a good meal and some drinks they settled into comfortable chairs and relaxed. There was a general chat and a rough idea of what Sam was thinking emerged.

After quite some while Bruce suggested they all go to another friend's later in the week. This man was an experienced boss in the film trade. Through that he had been to locations in nearly every part of the country and had many details in his head. After the usual social remarks he gave Sam a list of good places he had come across and a few names of people to contact. Both Bruce and Wendy were very successful people, but they enjoyed sharing their good fortune with any they came across. All this gave Sam a good store of ideas and places to look at. Meanwhile Bruce sought out any other friends who might be of help.

Chapter Eight

Bruce and Wendy lived in Fulham off the parade of King's Road and north of the market. Chelsea was their expensive neighbour, even though that had the evil-smelling rubbish disposal wharf not far away. New King's Road had been specially built to give a quick journey between Hampton Court and the royal residence. Charles II wanted it to be just for himself, but his advisers spoke against that and he rather reluctantly listened. Through much of his reign this situation had occurred. In these present days dandies and oddly-dressed folk used it to show themselves off. When that monarch ruled there had been market gardens all round there, but these had then been built over. This still left good soil and the physic gardens behind their old walls. Bruce and Wendy Rawlings had their own which could be admired through the French windows. The weather was definitely getting chillier, but it was pleasant enough when our visitors arrived.

Sam and Goldi went on the Underground to the old Walham Green Station (which unfortunately was later called Fulham Broadway). She liked making her own way to these places and not relying on lifts or taxis. Not long ago Americans didn't walk anywhere, although they would go on horseback. Then the brighter ones realised this left them them unhealthy and so they started jogging, which was to become very popular. Sam and Goldi reached the house around nine and were warmly welcomed. Inside it was almost silent with just a touch of Indian music from somewhere. The house looked plain from the outside, but was warm and welcoming inside. Goldi was warmly dressed, but soon took off the heavy layers. Among the other people a discussion had been going on about getting a good play area for the many local children. That stopped for the introductions, then carried on.

'Well if we are to get this play area we will have to get professional advice and put forward detailed plans. If we ask in general terms we get nowhere, as we have found in the past!'

That was agreed and most people offered to pay their share of costs. That ended their formal business then there was mainly a lot of chat among the younger women on bringing up their children. That did not interest Goldi, but he could not avoid hearing much of it.

They were given refreshments and let all the hubbub pass them by. To be in this pleasant place was enough for them for the present. One of the women was introduced to them. Caroline was a social worker in Balham. Sam asked her a few questions as Wendy moved on. Their host asked if Goldi would like to look round their garden and he was pleased to do so. It was just about dark, but solar lights made it pleasant. Past the lawn there was a whole range of ripening fruit and maturing vegetables. The peach tree which got the sun, but no rain, was loaded and Goldi really enjoyed a peach. They also shared a bunch of black grapes from the greenhouse. Coming in he smelt the lavender as well. After a word with Sam he went for a walk by the river. He found his way to the Embankment where he had a couple of stiff drinks. He went by Turner's house and across Battersea Bridge. All this was very much to his liking. One large statue said it was of Sir Hans Sloane. That was close to the physic gardens they had passed earlier. Now feeling a bit tired he thought he had better get back. He'd just have five minutes on this quiet bench first. He was soon asleep.

Police Constable Tompkins was training a new policewoman nearby. He did not enjoy this job, it was a long night. Janet wasn't bad-looking compared to some he had known. Now they were passing a quiet spot when she heard a noise which startled her. She then saw Goldi and told Tompkins.

'What are you kipping here for?' Tompkins asked. A snore was the only answer. Now our PC did not want to lose face, so gave Goldi a shake. Immediately Goldi sprang to his feet. He never liked getting caught unawares by anyone.

'It's not the ghost of Sir Thomas More,' the girl said, showing off her history pass at school.

'Well, judging by his clothes he *is* a Man for all Seasons.' Tompkins put on his most official voice. 'You know you are not allowed to sleep in a public place after dusk I suppose?'

Goldi of course knew nothing of the sort, but did not like the tone of voice. After a tense few moments Goldi was asked to accompany Tompkins and Janet to the Police Station.

Chapter Nine

Detective Constable Nixon climbed the steps of Walham Green Police Station wearily. He then went into the canteen for a cup of tea on this so-far quiet shift. He was a bachelor which was not common in the force. Through Christmas parties and the like they were thrown in with nurses from the local hospital, sometimes the same ones for years. Even if there was no lust on either side this familiarity often started off a courtship, then the 'victims' woke surprised to find they were married. Generally it paid financially to marry especially if the couple lived in police accommodation for some while. Nixon had in the early days hoped to reach at least Superintendent but that had not happened. He might have done better getting into the Kensington station where things of a higher level happened. In the midst of these rather gloomy thoughts he was approached by PC Burleigh. This long-serving man still looked like a pale teenager. He now said Nixon was wanted to help with an odd customer.

When he got into the interview room he looked at Goldi for quite a while, then asked the constable, 'What's he meant to have done?'

'Nothing as far as I know, except fall asleep on an Embankment bench.'

That did not sound much, but you never knew what might develop. Karl Marx had never been any trouble when he read about British working conditions around 1813. He had just sat in the British Museum Reading Room doing that in silence.

'Why am I needed now?' asked Nixon.

'Well, he doesn't speak proper English and can't tell us where he lives. Sam and Wendy is about all we understood. We do not need him here all night. He might start being a real nuisance if he wakes up properly.'

Goldi was beginning to get very annoyed. If these people had left him alone he would likely have woken up before long fairly sober, then found how to get back home. Now Nixon suggested Goldi try to write down his address, but Goldi said Sam did any writing he needed. It seemed odd that a mature man like this needed someone to write for him, thought Nixon, getting impatient.

Now a bit testily he asked, 'Now does this bloke Sam own the flat?'

'No, Sam is a girl it seems.'

They then carried on asking Goldi questions which confused him, but he managed to tell them the flat was owned by Mr Goldberg. Well that makes life a bit simpler anyhow thought Nixon. He then decided to contact Goldberg and get him to call in and collect Goldi. Then Goldi told him Goldberg was in the US at present. Irritated, Nixon then tried another tack. 'Now then Sir maybe you could tell us what your profession is?'

Goldi said he did not have a profession, but was used to farming and fishing at sea or in rivers. After this Nixon kept it all as simple as possible and so got a good deal more information.

'Can you do all that around Golders Green?' he asked in amazement.

'No, but I could back in Hokkaido.' While the others looked at a loss Goldi said, 'Can you ring Sam and get her to collect me?'

That was the obvious answer of course. They then looked under the Goldberg name and soon came up with a number. 'Well we will try it, but if she can't come round you will have to spend the night in the cells.'

When they said he would get a good supper and breakfast Goldi agreed that was a good idea and to leave the phone call until later on tomorrow. Relieved, Nixon then went out in search of some real villains.

Walham Green Police Station had only been built ten years earlier, so its facilities were the best around, almost civilised. Instead of having bars the windows of the cells were made of tough, thick glass bricks. Each also had a reasonable washbasin, toilet and bed. One of the policemen showed Goldi to it, then left him until breakfast time. The fairly hard bed was more to Goldi's liking than a soft one would have been so he slept very well.

The desk sergeant was contemplating his favourite thought – his retirement in less than five years' time. He might be able to afford a nice place in Spain. He was certainly not thinking of a place in the wet Lake District like that dreamy poet! This was interrupted by Sam on the phone. She had just got home and heard the message on the phone. She would not come out now, because as they said it was late. She was then amused to hear that Goldi was already snoring well! The next morning she set out for Walham Green and soon found the Station. She was not in a very good mood, so the duty sergeant did not make any jokes.

111

Instead he sent one of the constables to see if Goldi was ready. Goldi came in with a happy smile on his face, but her expression soon stopped that developing. She was really both pleased and annoyed to see him. 'There is nothing to smile about,' Sam said. 'I'm just annoyed.'

Secretly she was pleased to see this take effect, but he was still far from worried. The policemen present were not enjoying the atmosphere either, so Sam was soon allowed to take Goldi home.

Chapter Ten

Goldi was beginning to find that England had quite a few things in common with Japan. The main difference was the seasons and the past history of their peoples. The English could best be summed up as being not more civilised, but more experienced in worldly ways. Until the late 1880s Japan had been isolated even if its armed forces did sometimes go off and overrun parts of its much larger neighbour, China. Britain had been overrun and mainly pacified by the Romans so far back that it had soon become a part of the Mediterranean area, even if not its weather. Since then being very much a ship-orientated nation it had spread its trade and ideas all round the world. Not always for good effect however. What suited a damp, cloudy island was often not right for distant barren areas like Egypt or Australia. However not all its people travelled the globe. People such as those in the soggy clay of Sussex found it hard to go much more than a mile in wet weather. And the people of Cornwall or far Wales had very little in common in terms of either habits or language.

The Japanese, who lived in a much nastier island, slowly spread and pushed out those like the Ainu, or slowly absorbed them and buried their history.

Sam had some time back worked out a list of places

to look at for Goldi, and now started closer inspection. She picked up a four-wheel drive when they got north of London and set off. They had seen local places first like Emsworth which would have been all right, except it was crowded out all summer with small hire boats. Something like that, but with just working ones would fit the bill.

They had many false leads and were getting very frustrated until they reached Aldeburgh where the festival was under way. Sam appreciated the cosmopolitan group who seemed to enjoy the odd music. She then asked around and finally got them to the nice town of Louth further north. Here she took rooms for them in the good hotel, then proceeded to investigate all the likely quiet, working spots on the coast.

Sam now took him into a Louth estate agent's who had been recommended to her. He patiently listened to all the places down south and their faults. He then said, 'Well you will not be surprised the place I am going to recommend is also not perfect. As you have found out no place that has natural or man-made drawbacks is going to be just what you are looking for. However I think you will find this one is the nearest and not too far from here. Luckily the forecast somebody made of a Labour leader getting his way after the last war has not been fulfilled. They said he wanted all this country to be covered in miniature stately homes for the masses. Saltfleet is not like that at all.' This had been a very prosperous place, with large warehouses and a good, clear channel out to the sea. But over the years the currents had changed and now it was almost silted up and only something like a punt could get out. These would however be turned over much too easily by the strong prevailing wind that affects all that east coast. They were also told that the agent there would give them papers on a property that had been on the market for some time and was at present owned by a Mr Fairway. He thought that was because the asking price was too high, but Sam surprisingly did not seem worried about that. He then led them in his car, but left them to speak to the seller alone. They were both then delighted to see this well-looked after place was called 'The Tudor Inn'. Mr Fairway had bought it when it was very run-down, but then had spent a good deal of money on its renovation in the confident hope of taking in many good-paying guests. However he had been disappointed in that this never happened. His hope was now he might get some of that money back by getting rid of what had turned out for him to be a 'white elephant'. They were given a good light lunch, then Mr Fairway showed them round. They both liked what they saw and Sam said she would likely buy it, but would have it surveyed to be on the safe side. They then drove back to Louth in a very good mood where the estate agent said the survey could be done well and very quickly by someone he knew. Sam was in such a good mood that they changed over to a double bed-room, went to bed early and both enjoyed very good, long-lasting sex. With them both being quite mature there were not the problems that often plagued couples new to this delight.

Sam said Goldi could use whatever part of the place he wanted. He had soon decided the luxurious suites were not for him. He had looked at the staff accommodation and that was his choice. The harder bed and more spartan style were for him. That would leave all the rest for Sam's dad and any guests he wanted to entertain here. Now Sam said, 'I've been thinking

115

honey. We'll have to establish some sort of relationship if you are going to spend all your future time in Saltfleet.'

'I don't understand,' he said. 'We have this relationship.'

'Well in the London flat or even Manchester people do not concern themselves with other people's lives, even if the door of their apartment is right next to their neighbours, but in a smaller place like this everybody soon gets to know all about their neighbours' affairs, even if it is just from what the postman delivers.'

'Hmm, couldn't we say we are married?'

'No dear, because I won't be around all the time and then the locals would wonder where I go and what I'm up to.'

'Would that matter?'

'Not much, but I think it would be better if I let people believe you are a writer and I am your devoted secretary. That would give enough reason for me going off at all times.'

At first Goldi did not see much need for this, but after she explained some more he got the idea. However then he saw other problems. 'But I can only just about write my name!'

To which Sam replied, 'That is why I am getting you a good tape-recorder.' She then went on to explain roughly how that would work. Goldi was doubtful, but agreed to it. After this they had a lie-in before they walked round the smart little town and lunched. She thought the place looked big and busy enough to supply all their main future needs. After an enjoyable lunch they had another quick look round Saltfleet. She did not expect any difference, but then was surprised. It was low tide when they got there and they went to look at the sea channel. They thought a hovercraft would be the only vessel that could operate there, however they saw tractors moving about. Goldi could not at first see what they were doing, but he saw there were three moving slowly forward together. As they did so the drivers were looking about them. If he came to live here he would soon find out.

'If you lived here you'd need some sort of craft wouldn't you?' Sam said to him.

'Yes, a rowing-boat would do to start with. I would like to build myself a bigger one this time. I could do that over the winter if I had enough space.'

Further along they came upon an elderly man pottering about with a small cabin cruiser, so they stopped for a word. Mr Buxted was quite ready for a chat and among other things told them of the Roman road that passed nearby and also the fourteenth-century manor house. This area seldom got crowded because of the lack of decent water or open beaches. Some came over from Louth and then generally used the nearby inn. Only a few caravans were ever permitted and that suited the locals. After going on a bit more they went back to Louth, then Manchester. There they told Abe of almost all their doings. He promised to get the inn checked over very quickly. If the report was okay he would then arrange the money needed and also any work needed. They thanked him then made their way to their separated beds.

The day before Abe had brought the Tratskis to the hotel for an evening meal. After, while they were dozing, he told them some of the history of the rapid growth of Manchester. Abe enjoyed that sort of thing even if they were not taking it all in. Esther had also been doing some research but from a more personal angle. He told how the city's prosperity grew from King Cotton and how much of that was used by the more

117

thoughtful to establish the College of Music and also a fine orchestra and the *Manchester Guardian* which later became just the plain *Guardian*. 'This unlovely workshop helped to make Britain great,' he finished. When Esther raised Karl Marx's stay Abe was not so happy. She added that not only had the Communists oppressed the Jews, but also several czars. He retaliated with an opposite example. 'When the American Peabody came and saw the squalid conditions most labouring English lived in he did not write an agitating book. Instead he supplied the money and drive to build the Peabody Buildings which although now very modest by present standards were a genuine revolution in their heyday.' Here Esther tactfully let Abe have the last, winning word.

The visitors now spent a couple of days in Manchester before going back to Saltfleet. The Tratskis were thrilled when they heard of the plans, and that they would still be able to see the Greenbergs without too much travelling. This sounded a very satisfying outcome. They hoped it would all work out and Sam and Goldi would be happy there. Soon after this the trio returned to London for a while and carried on as before.

They did not have to wait long for the result of the survey. The main conclusion was that the property was basically sound. The sale then went through very quickly and then they concentrated on getting the revised layout they both wanted. That led to a rather long discussion but Goldi achieved most of what he wanted. This was that his part, like the main building, was only accessible by the keyholder. However there were two bedrooms in this part if Sam wanted to share with him and this gave them and her family choices.

When that was complete they went up together and decided how they wanted their part furnished.

On a cold January day Sam and Goldi finally moved into the now completed place. Abe was busy elsewhere, but he would open his part with invited friends when he was able later on. Sam had got Goldi a special key which he used to open their front door and he then carried her up to a bedroom where they continued to celebrate for some time. (They could not very well have done that if there had been a joint celebration opening with Abe.) Sam had added some very attractive plants to his list and made arrangements for them to be looked after when she was not around. All this made the place very welcoming. Some nice coffee was drunk in comfort as they recovered from their exertions. Apart from the essentials Sam had got some very nice prints that were good scenes of Japan and also a small study laid out where Goldi could record items that might be worth printing up later.

Sam had thoughtfully arranged for a nice lot of food to be sent. They then had a good meal and drink before celebrating again in front of a nice big log fire.

The next day they went into Louth again and got a large amount of supplies, much of which went into the big, new deep-freeze. The drinks went into a new sideboard nearby. They then visited an oldish couple whose son had recently married and gone with his wife to live in Australia. As he was their only child the contact knew this would leave a big gap in the couple's lives. The husband was also recently retired so in a similar state. Sam accepted the couple's offer of tea and biscuits, then got down to the object of this visit. She told them that Goldi was a writer who wanted

119

peace and quiet to do his writing when he was not getting his exercise going after lobsters and the like. She was his secretary, but would often be away in London and elsewhere. While she was doing this would the old couple (mother mainly) take care of Goldi's cleaning, washing and so forth? She would also like them to keep the place clean and if necessary contact anybody including herself in emergencies. Because of Goldi's poor English that would be a big help. She would give them a key and make it well worth their while. This was readily agreed to and a sum of money handed over, and they went happily on their way, pleased things had gone so smoothly.

Later that evening they enjoyed an even better celebration meal, as Sam had got used to using all the new kitchen equipment. After they celebrated this day by going to bed together and having a good, solid sleep. In the morning however they made love on a bearskin rug she had secretly bought. Really Goldi with his religious beliefs did not like doing this, but realised that this was one one of the few ways she was showing ignorance, so said nothing. However, he gave her a very rough going over which secretly gave her quite a thrill. Now she prepared to go back to London for quite a while, satisfied that after all that exertion he should be able to get a good deal of his knowledge and ideas down on tape. Goldi spent three days at that, but after went onto his real interest – learning how he could join the shell-fishing expeditions. He had guessed correctly that those experts would not want any stranger to learn their their ways, but he made use of Mr Buxted to get over that for him. Fred Lang was about Goldi's age and also quite a big fellow. He was now willing to help Goldi learn all he needed to join in with the others.

He said, 'What we mainly do is to go down with the low tide and collect crabs. If we spot anything else meanwhile we take advantage of that. Quite a lot of good-sized crabs get trapped in steep-sided holes where they are kept busy looking for victims. There is a steady market for them and it helps out many farmworkers on low wages.' Mr Buxted had already told Fred he could have extra money for his expenses which had helped to oil the works.

'You can come down with me this evening and see how it goes. A good pair of Wellingtons and gardening gloves you will definitely need.'

They parted on that agreement. Back home he always used something similar to Wellingtons, but they were made by men like him from strong, well-greased leather. Mr B. luckily had a good pair that Goldi could use until he bought his own. Mr B. however said his feet were larger than Goldi's. That however was an advantage, as he could also borrow long, oiled woollen socks until he bought his own. That seawater was never warm on this coast. That evening Goldi rode down hanging from the side of Mr B.'s tractor (a dangerous and illegal thing to do). He was soon enjoying himself collecting various-sized crabs. He had been told to leave the smallest so they could grow to a worthwhile size. Although he had never worked quite this way Mr B. was impressed how well he got on. Fred later spoke to Mr B. with a twinkle in his eye.

'That Sam says he's a writer and she's his secretary. She does not really fit that description, but as they are quite free with the money who are we to complain?'

Mr B. did not reply, but he had thought the same. It was noticeable that Goldi for all his lack of English easily got on with all the locals now. This was because they, like computer types or actuaries had their own language. One example of this was when he was introduced by some of the younger ones to their way of 'stunging'. Actually he had known this from his early days, but by an Ainu name. It consisted of standing quite still near a low-tide pool, then quickly stabbing any trapped fish. These were often really only 'bait-sized', but there was a market for them and the enjoyment was in having quick enough reactions. Back in Japan he had mainly practised it from a stationary dugout canoe. From those the fish they often caught were of a good eating size. He did not go into that here. An uncommon modesty seemed his best way forward in these at-present foreign parts. With Americans he could have been the opposite. From now on he was pleased to think he would be supplying all the fish or crabmeat he and Sam would want. This would be kept in their large freezers.

If he adapted his way of spearing fish from a stationary little boat he might earn more than the local farmworkers, but anyhow he intended to save most and then give some to Sam. He knew that she and her father did not need any more, but it was a matter of pride for him. If he supplied shell and other fish for them all plus some cash regularly he would not feel so much of a parasite. Goldi did not think all this out in such a detailed manner, but that is what it amounted to. He would enjoy making the boat which should help him to reach his goal.

One day when he was having a quiet walk along the beach on his own he saw someone he did not know in a bit of trouble. This man was trying to wrestle a large piece of timber through the small door of his boat-shed. With Goldi's added strength that was soon done. Once they had both got their breath back the grateful man asked Goldi how he came to be in this rather remote part of England. Slowly and with some difficulty Goldi gave him some idea. The man then said he was the local police constable in Louth. His name was Bob Parks and he was a bachelor. Goldi now realised they might have seen him in town, but would not have recognised him in uniform. He also thought it would be no bad thing to be a bit friendly with the local policeman in case he should get into any more scrapes. That was far less likely than in the past, but some unpleasant outsider could start it. He could not be the only person in the world who got in trouble, if he took too much drink! Although he had been born in Whitby Bob had been the local policeman here for twenty years and was soon coming up to his pension age. He would only be forty-seven then and would have plenty of energy left which he hoped to put to good use. He also saw that a friendly, working relationship with Goldi could be good. All the other local men, even if single had friends going back to their schooldays. Bob had got on okay with everybody, but with his position and being a former 'outsider' had never had close mates here. He told Goldi he also had built a boat for himself years back, but with more leisure had been looking forward to replacing it. If Goldi could help with any new ideas they could build two. Goldi would need to pay for his own materials, but Bob could supply a warmish, dry workplace in the coming nasty weather and any teamaking they needed. Goldi just said 'thanks' for now. Inside he thought it sounded ideal. They parted soon after this, but exchanged telephone numbers. Goldi did not like using those, but it would be useful.

As he made his way back to his home and supper Goldi thought how lucky he was to have come across this stranger just when he needed help. If this worked out as looked likely he would be able to make his boat, have Bob as his workmate and Sam as his partner at home most of the time. If he had tried to plan all this out in those now far off days back in Hokkaido he would not have thought it could possibly have worked out so well.

Not the end, but a new beginning!